FLATS

a novel by

RUDOLPH WURLITZER

with an original introduction by
MICHAEL GREENBERG

TWO DOLLAR RADIO
Books too loud to ignore.

This edition published by the Two Dollar Radio Movement, 2009.
ISBN: 978-0-9820151-4-8
Copyright renewed 2009 by Rudolph Wurlitzer.
All rights reserved.

Cover and author photographs by Lynn Davis.
Cover designs by Two Dollar Radio.

Flats copyright © 1970 by Rudolph Wurlitzer.
First published in 1970 by E. P. Dutton and Co., Inc, New York, and
Clarke, Irwin and Company, Toronto and Vancouver.

Quake copyright © 1972 by Rudolph Wurlitzer.
First published in 1972 by E. P. Dutton and Co., Inc, New York, and
Clarke, Irwin and Company, Toronto and Vancouver.

TWO DOLLAR RADIO
Books too loud to ignore.
www.TwoDollarRadio.com
twodollar@TwoDollarRadio.com

INTRODUCTION
by
MICHAEL GREENBERG

RUDOLPH WURLITZER OCCUPIES AN INTRIGUING PLACE IN AMERICAN literature. He writes from the extreme boundaries of experience and consciousness, yet brings to his work an intimate knowledge of U.S. history and culture – a knowledge of the corridors of power and privilege, of lowlife, decadent life, the contemplative life, and the lives of the stoned and self-imploding. His ability to combine these elements in a fictional landscape of dream-like intensity has made him an uncategorizable artist, in the best sense of the term. His characters dwell on the edge of an abyss. Wurlitzer presents this abyss matter-of-factly, which only serves to increase its horror. It can also be very funny. "We're tap dancing on a rubber raft," says one of the characters in his fifth, and most recent, novel, *Drop Edge of Yonder* (2008).

Critics have sometimes had trouble knowing where to "place" Wurlitzer. He is obviously a serious and ambitious writer, yet his profile is one of an outlaw who has flown under the radar of traditional American fiction. His first novel, *Nog*, continues to be read more than forty years after it was first published. Its partisans drink in the novel as an act of cultural defiance, the way Pynchon or Beckett are read in defiance. *Flats* and *Quake*, Wurlitzer's second and third novels, represent both a continuation and a deepening of the themes in *Nog*: the precariousness of identity, and the onion skin of the self that keeps revealing itself in a new guise as we peel away at it – all of which is conveyed through an inventive circular narrative strategy that doesn't "present" his characters so much as envelop their minds.

The barest outline of Wurlitzer's biography amounts to

a uniquely American portrait. He was born in 1937, to the third generation of an innovative American fortune – that of the Wurlitzer piano and jukebox – that was already in decline. At the age of seventeen he went to sea on an oil tanker that embarked from Philadelphia with stops in the Caribbean, Spanish Morocco, and Kuwait. "I had the lowest job on board," he told an interviewer. "Cleaning the engine room, that sort of thing. There was a lot to learn." Like William Burroughs, another outlaw writer born with a well-known family name, Wurlitzer had to overcome his advantages. As with Burroughs, the advantages were more of an idea than a reality: by the time his father died, when Wurlitzer was twenty-four, most of the family wealth had disappeared.

As a student in the English department at Columbia University he found himself in the orbit of Lionel Trilling and Jacques Barzun, influential men of letters of a traditional ilk with whom he felt little affinity. (A few years before Wurlitzer arrived at Columbia, Allen Ginsberg had also rebelled against Trilling's classical canonical view of literature.) Wurlitzer traveled to Cuba, enlisted in the army, did a stint in Majorca as Robert Graves' secretary, and then returned to New York, where his sensibility as a writer was formed amid a burgeoning, multi-dexterous art-scene that included Claes Oldenburg, Philip Glass, and the break-out jazz musicians La Monte Young and Ornette Coleman. His attraction to visual artists and musicians is telling. They were "breaking forms," Wurlitzer has said. "There was the sense that your work could take you anywhere. We had this invigorating feeling of permission to break the rules. It was spontaneous and fearless." One of the central ideas that he developed from this scene is that of keeping his characters in a heightened perpetual present, since the present is the only time that is real. Philip Glass's early minimalist compositions also explored this idea, as did Oldenburg's Happenings and experimental movies, some of which Wurlitzer took an active part in.

After the publication of *Nog*, in 1968, Wurlitzer began a parallel career as a screenwriter. He is one of the few serious novelists in the history of Hollywood who has been able, without compromise, to infuse his scripts with the same vision as his fiction. His most memorable movies – *Two-Lane Blacktop* (1971, directed by Monte Hellman) and *Pat Garrett and Billy the Kid* (1973, Sam Peckinpah) are road stories in the singular Wurlitzer vein. The frontier has disappeared, the psychic landscape of infinite possibility has closed down, and the characters "drift like blind men between the worlds," in a purgatory of emptiness and mayhem. In a mesmerizing scene in *Pat Garrett and Billy the Kid*, Pat Garrett fires his gun at a bottle floating in the middle of a river. It is a scene without explanation, completely outside of the movie's storyline, and indeed, outside of time. Yet it is or provides a concise image of Wurlitzer's most haunting themes: present time flowing endlessly; the impermanence of all things, cherished or not; and the violence and solitude of an open-ended America with a sense of futility and menace in its heart.

Fascinating as these movies are, the novels are where Wurlitzer's most potent and compressed material is to be found. Readers should be warned: a short period of initiation – twenty to thirty pages – is required to enter fully into the aura of Wurlitzer's world. Once you have earned your visa, the rewards are considerable. The territory you have entered will feel like a waystation on the road to nowhere, far from any conventional idea of "home." A feeling of disorientation may come over you, one that the author makes both exhilarating and disturbing. Any traditional sense of identity has been stripped away from the characters; their social positions have become irrelevant, as have their future and past. What interests Wurlitzer is not the adventures of the traveler but his state of being when confronted with a blank and unfamiliar landscape. Paradoxically, he deploys the metaphor of the open road – the metaphor of the Far West, America's myth of origin – to write about the solitude of interior space. In this sense, he is the opposite of a writer like Kerouac, whose chief concern is his characters' quest for identity. Kerouac is picaresque, Wurlitzer is existential. His road is a mirror of the mind.

Flats, for my money, is his most captivating novel. From its opening lines – "I walked a far piece. I'm sure of that. Not that I remember the old ways, signed directions." – the reader is thrust into a kind of zero degree of existence. It has been described as a "post-apocalyptic" novel, and though it does take place in the aftermath of some huge unspecified calamity, it is unlike any post-apocalyptic or dystopian novel I have ever come across. The frontier, such as it is, has shrunk to a matter of inches, and every inch is contested. The characters – all of whom have place names, such as Memphis, Flagstaff, Halifax, Houston – are preoccupied with the radically mundane: the contents of their pockets, their posture, cold, warmth, thirst, fire. From these animal concerns radiates a complicated philosophy of identity and intention. A kind of cosmic speculation arises from what is in front of the characters' noses. The most minute phenomena leads to existential speculation. "The turtle crawls toward me, away from the light. The tin cup reflects the fire. I could use an envelope, a connection between distances, the poisonous smell of the earth, the smoke or chemical waste that thickens or fades, gunfire to the south. I'm trying to delay a confrontation. I would rather maneuver among the politics of displacement."

Emblematic of this displacement is the way in which Wurlitzer's characters speak of themselves in the first person, then seamlessly shift to the third person, as interested observers of their own being. Sometimes the shift occurs within the same sentence, keeping the reader uncertain and identities in flux. This is not a literary mannerism or trick, but integral to the novel's mood. Much of the power of *Flats* derives from the neutral, almost documentary tone of Wurlitzer's prose. His sentences come at you, dart-like and short. "Omaha pushed again.

His teeth were clenched and he was sweating. The trunk moved six inches." There is little hierarchy of significance in Wurlitzer's world: a soup can label carries as much meaning as a storm, a scar, a gun, a man spitting blood. Far from being a throwaway item, the soup can label is a mysterious piece of evidence of the way things were before. The men read it as they would a sacred text, with a hint of sadness and longing. One of the pleasures of *Flats* is the way that the tangible and the abstract run constantly alongside each other, within easy reach. Wurlitzer nimbly dips into one, then the other, and on a certain level the novel is a dialogue between them. A Dixie cup, for instance, or a found bottle of tonic become objects of pathetic nostalgia, talismans of a lost innocence that never knew its own innocence when it existed. "Are there still beautiful places around?" Flagstaff asks Abilene who has arrived at their tiny area of shelter from afar, with possible news of the world. "No. There isn't even conversation," comes the answer.

I wouldn't want you to get the impression that we are in the realm of strict abstraction here. Wurlitzer is juggling a hatful of elements in *Flats*, including high drama, fueled by the presence of illness, destitution, a knife, a pistol, and the basic physical struggle to survive. The anxieties of the characters are unexpectedly moving. Facing imminent death, they take pains not to mention it directly. "I'm afraid of being stranded," confesses Omaha. "Don't let it ambush you," advises Flagstaff. In this broken new world, Wurlitzer tells us, "effect has long since been separated from cause."

Throughout the novel reference is made to a flying engine with a flashing blue light, droning overhead: the ubiquitous, unnamed predator. Leaving their little sanctuary in search of water, Houston is nailed by this predator, and finds himself trying to crawl to his death with a semblance of dignity. "It is always the same," he thinks. "We start so bravely with name and vision and it is the corrupt sound of our breathing that we are left with. I can't shake loose. I can't grasp the whole." Grasping the whole is a perennial quest in Wurlitzer's fiction, an unappeasable anxiety.

Near the end of this extraordinary novel, it began to dawn on me, with a shiver, that these multiplying place-name characters were really aspects of a single psyche, and that I had been traveling with the fragments of one consciousness all along.

While *Flats* occurs during the aftermath of a calamity, *Quake* takes place the day of a disaster: an earthquake registering 7.6 on the Richter scale that rips apart the thin social fabric that holds together Southern California. *Quake* is a more visual book than *Flats*, less cerebral, and is fascinating in its vivid depiction of unfettered human aggression. It is a powerful expression of American violence during the Vietnam war era that feels more urgent today than ever. One reads this novel with an open mouth, wincing at the total deterioration of decency that it describes, yet unable to put it down.

In 1969, Wurlitzer published an essay called "Riding Through," about the popular writer of Westerns, Louis L'Amour. Wurlitzer argues that the opening paragraphs of L'Amour's stories, when his characters are simply moving through space with no apparent destination, are masterpieces of minimalist prose. Only in this state of pure phenomenology then can true realism come to bear. When the plot kicks in, and the machinery of the potboiler takes over, L'Amour's novels become predictable and trashy. But in those suspended beginnings is something sublime. Wurlitzer's genius has been his ability to extend those L'Amour openings into full-length works of fiction. With the reissue by Two Dollar Radio of *Quake* and *Flats*, along with *Nog* earlier this year, readers at last have the opportunity to contemplate a unique and important American trilogy.

MICHAEL GREENBERG is the author of *Hurry Down Sunshine* and *Beg, Borrow, Steal: A Writer's Life*. From 2003-2006 he wrote the Freelance column in the *Times Literary Supplement*. He is a frequent contributor to the *New York Review of Books*.

FLATS

I WALKED A FAR PIECE. I'M SURE OF THAT. NOT THAT I REMEMBER the old ways, signed directions. I stopped. I would have crawled farther but the road gave out or I gave out. The horizon is limited, as if to say, I'm either resting in a hollow or crouching in a man-made hole. There are the usual impedimenta against nodding off: a dead oak, sticky tufts of brown grass. Two bricks. More, certainly, a garbage can, a complete list except that fatigue strangles my concentration. I know I stumbled through rubble, blown-up boulders or smashed statues. I moved in too slowly to distinguish clearly. But there is protection at the rear; weight, in any case, enough to sag against, to provide a look around. An engine throbs. Two blue lights move slowly into the darkness. I don't remember silence. The engine must have always been with me. After this space has been crawled through, the fear of inhabiting an area massaged, the promise of an event removed or established... There is no telling. I have no intentions.

Memphis nodded off.

Call me Memphis. There was that moment when I nodded off. I can refer back to that. But Memphis is the last place I started from. Not that I haven't located myself in a host of places: Toledo, Denver, Tucumcari, El Paso. But to tell it like it comes, as if from a direction, let it be Memphis: a root, a pretension. Memphis is not opposed. He accepts the garbage cans, bricks, railroad ties, the armatures of abandoned factories. The dead oak is a problem, whether to fully face it or turn away. What a shuck to invent a problem, now that a problem has occurred. Memphis will gather up the broken glass and smooth out a spot. The air smells of ozone. I should notice less. I should let the ozone notice Memphis. I started too fast. I never acknowledged that I wasn't on the road, that the journey has been forgotten. At least Memphis didn't slide into a beginning with his features, his brown suede shoes, his blue jeans and leather jacket. That is to say, my character. The ground is cold. It is coming on to night or winter. I would have preferred not to get into this, my last time out having ending long ago.

Memphis piled a brick on top of a brick. He threw away glass. I am not involved in a situation or any kind of combination. That I know of. Of course, I lost my way and lied the first chance I had, coming into the clearing. There were no blue lights approaching from the north. I haven't gazed at the sky in years. I was trying to get by, to manage a few remarks, to fill an empty space. The dead oak never interested me. I'm not trying to retrace my steps or find a guide. I saw smoke hovering over the dead oak and one distinction lead to another. I crawled in without announcement, without interest.

So Memphis found a campsite before dark. His gray Studebaker failed him a hundred miles back and he had walked a far piece and his feet bled. He crawled the last two miles. Then he staked out a vague perimeter with his pocketknife. He rolled a smoke. The area was full of wreckage, as if from a battle, and the horizon was hazed with chemical waste. Memphis was in the flats, west of the city. Nothing moved, nothing seemed alive.

I can't let Memphis wander too far. He expresses locations to himself, as if he knows where he is. I should do an exercise for control. Nothing flashy. But I rushed in before I became prop-

erly acquainted with myself. Minutes, hours passed unnoticed.
There was no transition, beginning having happened somewhere
else, the alarm mistaken for another noise.

A man sits on the smashed statue or broken boulder. He
wears a dark overcoat with fur collar, black trousers, unbuckled
galoshes. His face is long and skeletal with the ears and nose
pressing against the skull. His white hair hangs loosely over his
shoulders. He wears an Army pack. His gaze directs itself past
me, toward the dead oak. But I don't need a messenger or cata-
lyst toward a combination. I need Memphis to juke around without my own presence being increased or decreased.

"Do you have news?"

His question comes slowly from half-parted lips. He is very
old. He sits on the smashed belly of a concrete horse. I can distinguish separate remains of the statue: a bearded chin, an upper
arm, eight inches of sword in a clenched fist, a prancing leg.

Memphis approached the stranger with great delicacy. The
stranger was weary to the edge of collapse, his clothes torn, his
face and neck bloody, his hair matted with mud:

Memphis spoke softly:

"Come in and sit."

The stranger walked over to the dead oak and sat down,
removing his pack and resting his back against the trunk:

Memphis spoke again:

"You've been a distance. How about a fire?"

"I could use a fire."

Memphis turned over the garbage can, setting it upright. He
broke off a limb from the dead oak and snapped it into kindling.
He dropped the kindling on the shredded paper that lay on the
bottom of the garbage can. He lit the paper and a dull glow
appeared.

I am not altogether ecstatic to see him despite or perhaps
because of his being on the way out. I knew he was waiting for
an invitation, a greeting of some kind. Perhaps I can make the
switch without breaking stride, although only a fool would have
that kind of confidence. That was a fantastic moment: Memphis
having long ago and forever misplaced his repertoire of opening
gestures and then going ahead with the attempt anyway:

"Come in and sit."

And then I clamped my hands together, for warmth or greeting. And then that statement about his coming a distance followed by the proposal of a fire. Never mind the tenuous effort,
the matches failing one by one. That is history. The last one took.
I am adequate, the fire having been managed well enough. And
so, I am not alone, I couldn't have continued without claims being made, on my attention if nothing else. There are two now.

The stranger spoke:

"Which way you headed?"

Memphis has done all he is capable of. But he has to go. For
sure. No one appreciates more than I the way he moved in and
staked out a decent campsite. But he is confused. He did it all
too fast. His cadences, his hesitations have stiffened. He verges
on repetition. There were moments when he lost control, when

he became too oblique even to himself. Granted, he sank into one place long enough to maneuver through the embarrassment of a beginning. I owe him for that, for the arrogance of first words. But there is a stench to him now, something fetid, almost stillborn about his investigations. A change is necessary. It has been decided to transfer to Omaha. Omaha was once an expansive and open town for me.

"Call me Omaha.
"Come from there. No, it was New York. Lucky to get out of New York. Spent most of four days getting to the river. Had to summer south of Twenty-third Street."

The stranger has been silent since the fire went out. He might be conserving his strength. I know I stared openly at him and then he closed his eyes. But I was awed by his severity as much as by his experience south of Twenty-third Street. I was not offended when he ordered me to put out the fire. Memphis was blind to spatial strategy. There is so much to do. He never noticed how cramped the space is, how exposed we are from all sides, how falsely intimate this declivity is. Memphis had no curiosity. He was certainly boring, operating as he was within a monotone. There were gestures he wouldn't allow himself. Only: here I am, I am here now and that's where I'm looking, straight ahead, standing here, at this time.

The stranger spoke:

"You went at the makings of the fire wrong, like your hands was detached from your body."

The sky turned black and heavy. Omaha sat with his legs crossed, staring at the stranger, who leaned against the oak twenty feet away. Omaha scratched vaguely at the ground with his penknife. In front of him and slightly to his left he could see the line Memphis had begun on first entering the clearing. The line was two feet long and ran parallel to the smashed statue. Omaha erased part of the line and then drew it in again. He did this several times until he let the line stay. He leaned back, as if exhausted.

The stranger spoke:

"It don't matter none to me, but I might be here the night. I'm partial to warmth. Been moving too long and not far enough. This might be the last fire. You went at the approach closed and tight like you wasn't in to letting the heat penetrate your skin. Noticed you dropped pieces of dead oak on wet garbage and walked away. No good."

"I only just got here."

Omaha stood and walked over to the garbage can. He rolled the can beyond the tree and dumped out the garbage. Then he rolled the can back to its original position. He smoothed the can out with the palm of his hand so that the inside was slick and clean. He wiped his hands on his pants and walked out to where he had dumped the garbage. He retrieved the drier pieces of newspaper and a three-foot branch from the dead oak. He rolled the newspaper into long strips and placed the strips crosswise in the can. Then he broke the branch into six pieces and placed the pieces two abreast over the strips of paper. He reached into his pocket and took out a box of matches. There were no matches inside. The stranger handed him a kitchen match which he lit against the can. He placed the burning match against the first strip of paper, holding the match between his thumb and forefinger until his finger burned. He slowly straightened up and then sat down.

The stranger spoke:

"Recollect I managed a fire once. I occasioned it with cardboard boxes and a broken door. Was right inside the shell of the house. I'm fading. Must have been twenty bodies that moved in to appreciate that burn. I didn't pay them no never mind. But no one ripped anyone off, you understand."

It is warmer. Omaha's posture has slumped further. The line no longer runs parallel to the smashed statue. I curved it toward the oak. There's some movement to the line now. Omaha's voice is less strained. There was almost strangulation with Memphis. I don't know where Memphis crawled in from but most likely it was from a small disaster. Omaha's voice flows with no dictations. That's a statement that Memphis could never have handled. He was too fallible, too self-indulgent. Omaha is not watching the score. He's just playing the points as they come up.

"Name is Flagstaff."

The stranger's voice was so low that Omaha had to lean forward to hear it.

"By way of El Paso, Carizozzo, Denver and New York. I can handle any news you might have."

Omaha emptied his pockets and spoke the contents to Flagstaff:

"Two used three-cent stamps. One pebble. One ticket stub directing the bearer to Section B, Row 7, Seat 4, Ringside $5.00. Union Hall. Friday, November 29th. One Heinz Vegetarian Beans Tomato Sauce label. One pencil stub. One matchbox with the cover scratched off and no matches remaining. One half an inch of folded tinfoil. Three one-dollar bills and two quarters…"

Omaha stopped reading. A blue light moved slowly overhead. An engine started and then hesitated and stopped. Flagstaff had leaned forward, his mouth loosely open, his lower lip protruding. When Omaha stopped reading, he leaned back and shut his eyes. Omaha fingered the objects that he had not mentioned. He took the cellophane off a package of cigarettes and rolled it up. There were many more objects, nearly twenty, and he herded them together with cupped hands.

I thought it better to hold off, to save what information Omaha has left. I don't want to use up any advantage he may have originated. Although he has no sense of the future other than a vague revulsion, as if from an idea. He feels the need to impart information. The act awakens an old hurt, an anxiety I can't control. The glow from the fire has expanded. Although Omaha is unable to look at the outline of Flagstaff's face, he can focus on a beer can halfway there.

Flagstaff opened his eyes. He looked directly at Omaha. His thumb and two fingers pinched tobacco from a leather pouch that hung from around his neck. He pushed the tobacco into a black pipe that was minus half a stem. When Flagstaff had lit and taken a long poke from his pipe, he looked up and spoke to Omaha:

"That's not your spot."

Memphis would never have gotten into this. He wasn't involved with following instructions. He was never taken in by someone coming on too fast. No, there was nothing greedy about Memphis. But there was nothing accommodating about him either. He was always coming or just going. It was never necessary for him to know what existed in front of him, about what there was to do. The hell with Memphis. Flagstaff didn't

offer me a smoke. It is his hold on silence that Omaha is beginning to resent. But I don't want to become involved in priorities.
Although Omaha made the fire. I'll leave the area beyond the
can to Flagstaff. He can have the oak. It's dead anyway. Omaha
will take the smashed statue. It offers more protection.

Omaha drew a line with the knife, toward the smashed statue.
Then he joined the line to the line Memphis had created. He
stood up and smoothed out his jacket. He licked his upper and
lower lip. Then he stepped backward ten feet, keeping his eyes
on Flagstaff's galoshes. It was a slow retreat, taking nearly forty
minutes after all the pauses were accounted for.

Flagstaff can have the contents of my pockets. He might receive them as a gift. If he reciprocates I'll refuse. That will give
his gesture too much weight. Omaha will shift into the offen-
sive, no doubt, and gain more control around his own space. I'm
coming around. When Omaha presses forward… I've lost the
thread. These last moments hint toward consequences. The fire,
the sky, my brown suede shoes, are less accessible. Something
must have taken their place. I must be whispering to myself because the throb of the engine breaks in everywhere. But Omaha
is definitely here, having moved back. I am confused about the
usual paraphernalia of names and directions. I have to pretend
Omaha is moving on, toward the city, even though I might have
come from there. Or is that Memphis? These are tight areas, to
be sure, involved as they are with definitions. I feel a mixture
of nausea and calm. I have experienced these moments before,
when the air expires and gives out with a rush, as if the elements, or any element at all, are not centered within me. Omaha
is looser. He's less bent to the problem, he's able to forget more,
although there was that moment when he was strategically involved with Flagstaff.

The fire glowed. Omaha sat twenty feet from Flagstaff, staring past the dead oak. He raised his arm over his head, as if in preparation to speak, but then let his hand drop slowly into his lap. He hummed. The sound that emerged was a low one-note. He stopped humming. Flagstaff looked at Omaha without expression. After a long silence, Flagstaff spoke:

"We don't have to hold this space. But I'm partial to a few of the old moves. I'm not going to say there is only this one space but this is where I'm sitting. You get the drift. There's two kinds of smoke rising: from the pipe and from the can. I'll take either one. Listen I ain't got but so many matches left. So I'm sitting here like I'm sunk in a beautiful deliberation. Are you ready for that?"

Omaha crackled the cellophane before he answered:

"Every morning I wake up and say I'm going to have hot cereal and I never have any. I'm not too well wrapped."

Flagstaff stared without blinking at Omaha. He replied:

"Best to let yourself get pressed into the prone position and make it from there. If I was you."

Omaha tried to meet his gaze but failed. He concentrated on the beer can and then on the spread of objects he had abandoned.

We must be involved in some kind of plan or rapprochement; at the least a discussion about the effects of forgetting the purpose. But Omaha has no plans. He wants to put in his time as if the time hadn't run out. He doesn't need to adopt a strategy of being somewhere together with whoever is around. He has nothing particular or immediate to communicate. He has no information that he has not struggled with too much, that has not already defeated me.

Omaha stood and then advanced. He stopped before his possessions. He sat down and spoke aloud an inventory:

"Gray Studebaker, dead oak, choking engine…"

He was unable to continue. His fingers moved restlessly over the objects in front of him.

Flagstaff was heavy. The fire was the least of it. I don't mind building a fire. But what he said was coiled too tight. He's been ripped off so much that no one's at home except a few dull edges. Omaha is passing through. If it gets too rigid I can take ten steps back to Memphis. It's a dodge to come on like that. Omaha keeps sinking into the first person like warm mud. He's always rescued in time. As if I set that up without letting myself in on it. The third person handles the changes, keeps me from getting popped. I don't want to knock the third person. I like to travel there. It avoids stagnations and the theatrics of pointing to myself. But I'm not into making distinctions about who comes along. Any pair of traveling shoes can kick the switch.

Omaha opened his mouth to speak but no words came. The fire had lost its glow. A calm lake stretched between Omaha and Flagstaff. The silence and darkness had come together and become heavier. The lines scratched on the ground were still visible even on top of the lake. The lines crossed each other in a series of X's but the whole formed the beginning of a circle. Flagstaff had opened the flaps of his pack. His hand had reached inside the pack but had not yet withdrawn. His head lay upon the trunk of the oak, his eyes staring at the dead branches.

A blue light moved slowly across the sky. Omaha lay leaning on one elbow, a finger dipped into the earth.

I want to cut in here. I don't want Omaha to become a master of a dazzling diversity of techniques. He's ailing. All the signs point to that. An ache, as if from loss, permeates each bone. He doesn't have time for trick stuff. He's trying to realize a focus before everything fades or changes too fast. If I could remember a story I would tell it. That always helps to hold ground, to pass the time. If only Omaha knew that it's not all bad here. The noise has fallen off. The ground is smooth enough. He's thirsty but I can put that off. Something specific is bound to happen, or I am bound to recognize… No, that's all wrong. The fire is fading. Stories in the dead of night are always fabricated, pointing to relief, to a way out, to a cozy direction. Omaha tries to reach out, to know someone is sitting out there. But the effort has already made him obsolete… Omaha can no longer see Flagstaff. Flagstaff might not be able to see me. He might assume Omaha has split. But no doubt there are certain maneuvers that are even now directing me toward him. I feel that Omaha and I won't be partners much longer. Speaking out, he will fade; the rhythm of a statement building him up or sliding him off will make him oblique, a name to be dropped. I can't stop. Flagstaff might be waiting for a reply. I could scratch a deep line with the knife pointing directly into Flagstaff. That would be in the nature of an overture. Omaha needs to draw this moment out a little, to hang on to this voice. I just got here, the action will always come, I'm getting into the voice, it's no longer in the top of the throat, it has shifted down, to the stomach, toward the lower regions. I don't know enough about saving gestures. Omaha is afraid of expansion as much as he is of contraction. He is afraid to stop talking. He is afraid to look directly at Flagstaff. He is afraid to ask for water. He is afraid to go to sleep. He is afraid to move about. He is afraid to move on. He is afraid of what is behind and in front of him. He is afraid to last the night. He is afraid to acknowledge what he doesn't know. He is afraid of any concentrated act. He is afraid to set up a plan, to make a move that ensures a result. Omaha is a drag. I am unable to bring it all together, to say something clear, that I can remember. If Flagstaff could break through, the whole area would be helped out. Of course, he is probably frozen within his own reflections. Omaha is certainly rigid and inaccessible... That's too strong. More than one transition is too much for Omaha. And Omaha has eluded me. After all, I never said what he looks like, how he presents himself, where he is going. I'm over my head. I need a task. A task would give a focus, prevent distractions. To keep on is a task. The first person causes despair, blow Omaha's cover. I have my eyes closed. And yet I can't stop... Omaha has opened his eyes. I knew there would be too much said, that the order of this space would be somehow profaned. Omaha can't follow what directly happens or does not happen. And that is what I am after but I can't handle it.

Omaha spoke:

"I'm passing through."
Flagstaff replied: "I know you're passing through."
"How do you know I'm passing through? I might want to stay on."
"You're passing through because you let the fire die. And because you said you were passing through."

Omaha lay still but kept an eye on Flagstaff. The fire had receded into the black orb of the ash can. The lake had disappeared. Flagstaff took a candy bar out of his pack. He unwrapped it and broke it in half. He ate one half and put the other half into the pack. He smoothed out the wrapper. Then he stood up and walked over to Omaha's possessions. He lay the wrapper next to a rubber band and a pencil stub. Then he walked back to the oak tree and sat down.

He could have thrown me half the candy bar. Omaha is joined to the situation, I'm ready to admit. Although hopefully no motives have crept in pushed by the mad need to speak. But doesn't Flagstaff see that? Perhaps he has made a pact with himself not to consider the other half of the candy bar; any half that doesn't involve his immediate needs. I understand but I'm not ready to suffer through someone else's schemes. Who knows what he has in mind for this space? Perhaps he's planning to build and Omaha is in the way. Perhaps a dream pushes him, an urge to venture forth from the ruins behind him. That's too poetic, too fragmented. I'm not in touch with any of that.

Omaha spoke toward where he imagined Flagstaff was sitting:

"Tell me the truth. How is it going with you?"

There was no reply. Omaha sat up and put both hands over his face. He rocked back and forth. A moan escaped from between his teeth. He spoke again:

"You walk in and sit down and tell me where you're from. But you don't know where you are or where anyone else is. Listen, I was here first. You didn't exactly acknowledge that. What is this, some kind of imposition? I'm at a disadvantage. Everything has fallen apart behind me. I walked through that. I come from Omaha, after all. I want to get it straight. You order me to build a fire and I build a fire and then you complain that I let the fire die out. You pace around and shout at me about the collapse of everything. You take over. Okay, take over. Direct all the traffic. I don't care. But then you eat half a candy bar and don't offer the other half. I haven't eaten or talked to anyone in days. And I'm thirsty. It's something like that. I think that's where it's at."

Omaha waited until his pulse was slower. Then he stood up and slowly bent to check out his arms and legs. He stepped toward the oak tree. There was no sound or movement from Flagstaff. He stepped farther. He passed Flagstaff and touched the oak tree. He broke off two of the dead branches and split them into small pieces with his foot. He put the kindling into the garbage can and blew on the embers. Two lines of flame slowly emerged. He stared at the lines until his eyes blurred. Then he fell to his knees and crawled to where he imagined he had originally started from.

Flagstaff spoke from the darkness:

"You built the fire."
"That's right, I built the fire and I kept it going."
"You staked out this space. You came in and began to wait it out."
"I was here and I more or less got involved with staking out this space."
"It doesn't matter whether we're going anywhere together."
"We're not going anywhere together. You're sitting over there and I'm sitting over here."

Omaha's vision cleared. He stared directly before him. The fire had increased the perimeter of light and now Flagstaff's outline was visible. Flagstaff sat cross-legged, lifting his pack in front of him with both hands. He let the contents fall to the ground. Omaha was able to distinguish a silver pistol, a large roll of gauze, a red bottle, a tin cup and what appeared to be a small, soft-backed turtle.

I don't like the way things are going. At least Memphis was involved with simple particulars. I return to Memphis because I don't know how to go on with Omaha. Memphis was straight about his own fallibility. But Omaha is unable to acknowledge that he can't handle particulars, that he is unable altogether to expand a given context. Of course, he lacks will. If that was only the problem. I am more distant with Omaha, more separate from his actions, as they seem more necessary. These observations aren't enough. Omaha could use an object. They are spread out before him but his fingers don't reach for them. Flagstaff has initiated a dialogue. At least to Omaha. I don't take sides. Somewhere, in one of us, control lurks. The distance has been arranged, the fire expanded or contracted, the conversation begun or terminated. The turtle crawls toward me, away from the light. The tin cup reflects the fire. But that is only addition. There are a few recent moves that I haven't accounted for. Like Flagstaff taking a leak against the tree. Flagstaff advancing within a foot of my objects and adding a crushed Dixie Cup, a handkerchief and a Band-Aid. He peered at me, as if to speculate, and then moved quietly back. Flagstaff taking off a galosh and then a shoe. Omaha digging a small hole and burying an eraser. Omaha biting his lower lip so that it bled. Omaha noticing blood on Flagstaff's neck and an oil-stained rag around his shoulder. I'm not keeping what's available firmly packaged. I could use an envelope, a connection between distances, the poisonous smell of the earth, the smoke or chemical waste that thickens and fades, gunfire to the south. I'm trying to delay a confrontation. I would rather maneuver among the politics of displacement. Omaha is so facile about sliding away from whatever tempo has been established. Nothing picks up, nothing rushes forward toward an exclamation or conclusion. And yet there is danger and Flagstaff is not to be trusted. I must need these cheap asides as much as Omaha needs the slick device. It's faster that way, to fake the hesitation, the accommodating gesture that initiates a step forward to get to a step backward. Omaha could never stand still, was never into homesteading, sinking down or chewing his food.

Omaha extended the line with his penknife. The line pointed toward the turtle, who had stopped a few feet from Flagstaff. Omaha dropped the penknife into the pile in front of him and closed his eyes. The length of sound overhead increased. His breathing quickened. He opened his eyes. The fire glowed. There were several new objects in front of him: a small pebble, a five-dollar bill, three pennies, a scrap of yellow paper and a handkerchief clotted with blood.

I feel anchored to the earth, the throbbing engine pushed down on me and there is a heaviness to my ass and my crossed legs. I can smell a slight dampness, a rancid odor, as if from rotting garbage.

Flagstaff spoke:

"I heard you sigh."
"I've been doing that."
"We have to get something established, to talk it over. I might be coming apart."
"That's too fast for me."

Flagstaff moved his legs. He lined up the cup and the pistol next to each other. He leaned his head back on the trunk and whistled, a tuneless one-note.

Omaha spoke:
"I'm not interested in doing any crossing over. I've traveled too far, too often. You stay over there and I'll hang in here. I've got enough to amuse me… Listen, I'm just trying to get through the night."

These last gambits from Omaha have been false, even ruinous. I expected more. I've been nervous, sure, but he doesn't have to plunge into banal comments and proposals. Flagstaff must have slipped badly. He's not sitting with any authority. Perhaps Omaha will hold his own after all. He wasn't taken in by that sudden plea for alliance. It's been a long time since he's messed with the problems of a common front. Not even Memphis was in to that. Flagstaff has definitely slipped. It's not that Omaha has come on, although he did manage to get the words out when hit upon. And Memphis, as Omaha knows and never gets tired of saying, would have been paralyzed in front of a barrage such as Flagstaff laid on. No word would have come forth from his paralyzed lips. This might be a setup, of course. He seduces me into thinking of Memphis and how things are so much better without him and before you know it he's sitting next to or behind me. That's lucid. That's concise. Omaha is on top of his own collapse, riding it down like a freight elevator. There are stories for him to tell. He can do it now, coming as he has from rape, murder, cannibalism.

Omaha scooped a handful of dirt and held it before his nose. He dropped the dirt on the pile in front of him. The fire had diminished slightly. Flagstaff sat motionless. There was no sound.

Something has to happen. Omaha shifted slightly and I cannot contend with that. I cannot remember my original spot. My eyes are drooping. If only Omaha could make the jump into what Flagstaff is thinking. For instance: Flagstaff eyed Omaha warily. He needed Omaha to fit into his plan. He moved a few inches closer to the fire, his hand reaching for the pistol. If he could control the space long enough for… Omaha can't make the jump. I can only handle what is directly in front of me and that has slipped away. Flagstaff has to be handled from here, without interest, without intent. Omaha can't sneak behind him and look toward myself, as if from Flagstaff's point of view. Although there are moments when Omaha threatens to swing into omniscience. But that's for relief, for balance. Omaha needs to state a resolution. No doubt Flagstaff is making an effort along those lines, to put it together, to say what it is all about, so that nothing will happen. He's probably as afraid as Omaha to open up the space. Flagstaff's hand circles warily behind his back. I don't know why.

Omaha stared at the tin cup in front of Flagstaff's foot. The sole of the foot was black, the toes short and lumpy. The galosh on the other foot appeared huge in comparison. Omaha stood up. He wavered and walked two feet to his left and sat down. The fire had diminished. Omaha sat cross-legged, searching for the turtle which he was unable to see. Flagstaff stood up and stepped into the darkness behind the tree.

Omaha screamed:

"Don't go. Don't leave me."

Flagstaff walked into the circle of light and sat down in the same spot, leaning against the trunk of the tree. Flagstaff spoke, looking toward Omaha with squinting eyes:

"We can push over the tree and that will serve as a barrier. We need a barrier."

Flagstaff stood up. He walked slowly to Omaha and paused before him. He regarded him coldly. Then he bent down on one knee and picked up the penknife. He straightened, returning his gaze to Omaha. He gestured with the knife in a long sweeping arc.

"This space will be defined by twenty-five paces around, more or less."

Flagstaff walked back to his original spot, stopping every few feet to rest. He sat down and laid the knife gently among the objects before him.

Flagstaff is a lot older than I thought he was. I feel younger knowing that he's so old. The knife doesn't matter. Let him have the knife. It was that slice in the air that has changed everything. I thought he was drawing up the knife to cut his neck. Then he must have changed his mind and made that comment about the space. Omaha was caught napping. Twenty-five yards is claustrophobic but Omaha can handle it. The ground is smooth here, it's cooler away from the fire but my jacket is warm. I still have a few straight and curved lines before me, pointing nowhere in particular. I still have the smashed statue behind me. It's not too bad. Omaha has seen a lot worse. I even prefer it like this. Flagstaff's timing must be way off. He didn't make that gesture with any confidence. His arm floated and then dropped. It was enough for him to come close and move away. He encouraged a sense of enclosure. So that I can't remember walking a far piece to get here.

Omaha stood up and walked over to the oak tree. He pushed at the trunk, trying to make it topple. The tree gave slightly, leaning toward the earth. Omaha called to Flagstaff:

"The roots are dead clear through."

Flagstaff stood up and put his back to the trunk. His added weight moved the trunk a foot. Omaha pulled and Flagstaff leaned, although Flagstaff had obviously weakened and was breathing hard. The tree had been dead a long time and the

roots shifted easily. Flagstaff sagged to the ground, blood drip-
ping from his bandages, but Omaha continued to lower the tree.
Omaha stopped and read aloud the initials carved on the trunk:

"A.B… S.G… J.E… J.W… I.O… S.S… R.N… There are
more but I can't make them out. Fuck them. I'll read them
later."

Flagstaff sat with his arms around his knees, his head low-
ered. Omaha sat cross-legged, his arms folded across his chest.
They sat for a long time, staring at the fire. Finally Flagstaff
spoke:

"Read me some labels. As a favor."

Omaha returned to the pile of objects. He sat down and
picked up a label. He read it aloud:

"One Heinz Vegetarian Beans Tomato Sauce label. Ingredi-
ents: Beans, Tomatoes, Sugar, Salt Distilled Flavoring Spice. 7
Oz. Net Wt. 198 Grams. MFD. In U.S.A. by H.J. Heinz Co.,
Pittsburgh, Pa."

Omaha read two more labels:

"One Pencil: Bonded Lead Torch brand 505, Number 2…
One match cover: WHO CARES? A&P CARES! Every pur-
chase guaranteed to please or… your money back."
Flagstaff nodded. Omaha sat before the pile of objects. A
series of chills made their way through his chest and upper back
and he pulled the collar of his jacket up. He shivered but stayed
where he was.

Who is the enemy? Omaha has to decide. It is already too late, all that having been taken care of before he began, but I have to make a decision. I can't grasp why. But Omaha needs a common purpose, to get through the night or whatever is behind it. Memphis waits for me to return but that is impossible. I need to pull at the tree trunk. If we succeed in bringing the trunk down, we will establish a barrier. The enemy can be beyond the barrier. We will sit through this last protective period together. We will contract and squeeze this space and it will be something to do. It will be a way of waiting. A footstep is no longer the enemy. That is all over. It must be that we are the enemy and we have won.

Flagstaff spoke:

"We got to get the tree down."

Omaha stood up and walked over to the tree. Flagstaff was already leaning against the trunk, although his weight had ceased to matter. Omaha pushed and moved the trunk another foot. Flagstaff spat up blood, the spot fading into the earth. Omaha broke off the two remaining branches. The trunk was removed of its appendages. Omaha pushed again. His teeth were clenched and he was sweating. The trunk moved six inches. Omaha sat against the trunk and rested. Flagstaff tapped the tin cup against the pistol.

The fire will go out. Flagstaff and I moved the tree together. Omaha is exhausted but he is determined to continue. The fact that Omaha pulled and Flagstaff pushed and they moved the trunk gave him a tremendous lift. Omaha is broken, of course, but he is bent to a purpose even though he doesn't know what it is.

Flagstaff spoke:

"Where is the turtle?"
"He crawled off."
"We have to find the turtle."
"It doesn't make any difference."
"It makes a difference."

I forget where I am.

Omaha found the turtle underneath the head of the statue. The head of the statue was large and cracked across the skull. A piece of the cheek was missing. The eyes were hollow. The chin had a pointed goatee and the lips were pressed together in a military fashion, that is to say, forceful. Omaha glanced at the head and reached for the turtle. The turtle offered no resistance. Omaha sat on the horse's smashed belly and held the turtle in one hand.

Omaha and Flagstaff are no longer included together. That seems a regression. Omaha stares at the tree. There is an arrow on the trunk pierced by a heart. I don't need to discover images, certainly not to remember them. They float up, as if pushed by panic. I could manage one or two – I don't want to be a fanatic – but I prefer to stare.

Flagstaff straddled the trunk, his head sinking to his chest. He raised an arm a few inches and managed a shout:

"I'm going to ride this mother to the ground."
Flagstaff fell off the trunk. He lay on his side, one hand smoothing out the ground. Omaha walked over to the trunk and put the turtle next to the pistol. He stepped over Flagstaff and straddled the trunk. Flagstaff lifted a hand, as if to join him, his fingers brushing the bark. Omaha bounced up and down and together they forced the trunk to the ground.

Flagstaff should have a few more hours in him. He should be able to raise his hand again. Omaha will follow shortly after. He still straddles the trunk, which is nearly twenty feet long and two feet wide. Flagstaff plays with the laces of my shoe. The turtle has crawled a few inches toward the center of the circle. I am content to straddle the trunk, the fire warming my left side. But Omaha should return to my spot before his ability to locate himself disappears altogether. The chills are increasing. My left side is numb. Perhaps because the fire and thus the light has faded. Flagstaff has crawled a few feet from the trunk, possibly trying to recover his original spot.

Omaha broke the two branches into kindling and fed them to the fire. Overhead an engine droned. Omaha reached for the pistol and sighted it on the turtle, who had stopped near the pile of objects. Flagstaff lay sprawled on his stomach, his right arm underneath his face, his left arm flung forth. Omaha squeezed the trigger. There were no bullets in the chamber. He placed the pistol near the tin cup. He sat down with his legs crossed and stared at the ground in front of him.

Flagstaff spoke:

"Come through a swamp to get here. Up to my knees in mud and water. I was almost sucked under. Probably picked up the turtle there."
"If not there, somewhere."
"All right."

Omaha smoothed out the space in front of him, lifting the pistol, the knife and the cup and putting them down again. He drew a line around them so that they were enclosed. He pulled a button off his shirt and put the button between the pistol and the knife. He stared at the outline of the smashed statue. Then he picked up the knife and crawled forward. He sat and stared at a twig that lay outside of Flagstaff's circle of objects. He crawled to the twig. He stared at a strip of white plastic near Flagstaff's foot. He crawled to the strip of plastic. He drew a half circle around the strip of plastic and Flagstaff's foot. Then he crawled forward, toward Flagstaff's spot. He reached Flagstaff's spot and sat cross-legged, staring at the ground in front of him. He laid the knife next to the pistol and shut his eyes.

Omaha spoke to Flagstaff:

"I'm in your spot and you're in mine."
"Don't let it ambush you."
"I'm afraid of being stranded."
"Leather and rawhide are edible. Frogs, dandelions and pigweed. Bones will save you. Wild onions and mice. Anyone can build a lean-to. Nobody taking you away from your sources. Getting birds without guns. Insects and grubs, moths and mayflys. The woods aren't wet. No one here to choke off your sustenance. I'm tired."

The space between Omaha and Flagstaff no longer has my attention. Articles are no longer significant or pleasurable. There is a tin can three feet away, to my right. I can't make any arrangements. Omaha can't crawl farther. There are too many intersecting lines. They don't point anywhere in particular, that Omaha knows of. Flagstaff must be working up his own set of lines, perhaps an encompassing circle. I need to confess something, as if for relief, but Omaha has nothing to confess.

Omaha spoke:

"I don't feel you in front of me."

There was no reply.

Omaha picked up the knife and stood up. He shuffled outside the circle of light and sat down. He faced a low line of bushes several feet away. The knife had dropped behind him as he approached a sitting position. He groped for it but couldn't reach it. His back was to Flagstaff and the fire. He was unable to turn. He stared at a small stone. The smashed statue was to his right. He had never investigated the area to his left.

Omaha can't distinguish where one bush leaves off and the other begins. The knife must be in back of him. I am unable to turn around. There might have been too many images, too many changes for Omaha. He is not able to remember what he is looking for. I stare at a small stone. The small stone remains a stone even though its color becomes paler and its circumference smaller. If Omaha could walk to the bushes and beyond, everything would change. But he is played out.

Flagstaff spoke, his voice a whisper:

"Now I'm going to let the top part drop in front. To bypass is not practical. You understand that a down tree can get you over a ravine or a perilous stretch. I don't know exactly what I'm saying. I've been testing such footings for too long; the point is to secure handholds whenever they are offered. Seen the time when a low-hanging cloud would do me in. That isn't the point. But I was moving in those days."

Omaha sat with his back to Flagstaff. He stared at the bushes ahead of him. The knife was directly behind him. Flagstaff had fallen forward, his head touching the ground. An engine droned. A blue light blinked. Nothing moved around the half circle. The radius of the fire extended twenty feet. The light illuminated one side of the fallen tree and the back of Omaha's leather jacket.

I am aware that all this might be a cheap trick, that I might have been setting up an arrival as Omaha departs. Omaha has been tapping on any object that appeared in front of him. He has groaned. These delays, if that is what they are, haven't been handled well. Omaha is tired. He can't handle the increasing lack of attention. He can no longer pivot, as if to indulge in the swing or intersection of lines. But now that he is slipping away, has slipped away, he may attain purpose, fate even: he can be rounded off. But Omaha was a spin-off and I am too distracted to pronounce an elegy.

Omaha turned. Flagstaff sat cross-legged, staring at the objects before him. Several new objects had been added: three toothpicks, a black shoelace, a five-dollar bill and a red cigarette package. An emaciated man in a yellow rain slicker sat on the trunk. He was untying the laces of a GI boot. His boots were caked with mud, as were his khaki pants. His finely boned face was covered with a reddish growth of beard. His brown hair was long, falling to his shoulders.

I prefer the black shoelace lying across the toothpicks. The five-dollar bill should be placed in the red cigarette package.

In any case, Halifax decided that the wreckage before him needed to be arranged. Flagstaff sat cross-legged, staring at the objects before him. The stranger sat on the trunk. He had removed both boots and was warming his feet before the fire. Halifax picked up the knife. He scratched a line toward the trunk and curved it toward Flagstaff. Then he stood and walked over to Flagstaff. He touched Flagstaff on the shoulder with the tip of the knife.

"We have to get something arranged."
"There is nothing to arrange."

Halifax prodded him with the knife and he looked up.

"We have to get together on an approach."
"He's sitting on the trunk. Let him have his spot. I've been done in too many times along the way to reach out for some kind of opportunity. My stomach hurts."

Halifax placed both hands on the back of Flagstaff's overcoat and raised him to his feet. He guided him into the darkness where he whispered into Flagstaff's ear:

"We have to hold this space. You said we have to spread out from here. We have to establish who comes and goes."
"Way off. We don't have to decide on anything."
"You can't just go back and sit down."
"That's a low shot. I'm not trying to make it all come to me."

Flagstaff took half a candy bar from his pocket. He gave the candy to Halifax. Halifax ate the candy bar. Then Halifax and Flagstaff returned to their recent if not original spots.

There are no surprises in Halifax. Ships sail in and out of the harbor on schedule. The weather is dull and unspectacular. The economy is regular. But I must have taken Flagstaff by surprise. Halifax might embarrass all of us before he's done. This night is not like the last. But there's no use getting up a tingle. Effect has long since been separated from cause. I don't aspire to recollect. If Halifax could work up a little paranoia, some semblance of intensity, just to reach the dawn. That would help. That never helps. We will sit through this night together, whether we know it or not. There is nothing to notice. We have all been busted, whether we know it or not. There is nothing for Halifax to establish. So let the stranger warm his toes. Let him be the result of his own stumbles through the night. But I resent him. I resent him sitting on the log that Omaha felled, that I talked about. Halifax's words aren't that shiftless, they aren't that worthless that a stranger can walk in and crash on initials Omaha noticed. He won't help Halifax get through this night. He won't help him surrender the illusion of control. He won't help him establish a date or suffer time passed. I will have to refer to Omaha and perhaps back to Memphis for that.

Halifax crawled closer to Flagstaff. They faced the stranger. The stranger lay with his head on the trunk, his eyes closed. His feet were small. A dirty Ace bandage was wrapped around one ankle. The air had become harder to breathe. A blue light blinked overhead. There was no sound except for Halifax crackling cellophane from the red cigarette package. Halifax picked up the three toothpicks from the pile, handing one to Flagstaff and sticking one in the ground. He put the other in his mouth. Together they chewed on the toothpicks and watched the stranger.

Flagstaff whispered to Halifax:

"Recall a similar situation. Several springs ago. Referred to it then as a jerk-off. Took most of two days to get clear of that particular corner."
"He has the fire. Let him have the fire. It's not that cold. We have the statue. We can get behind the statue with the knife. That's strong. And the fire is bound to die out."
"I don't want to go that route."

How am I doing? Halifax has no way to answer. He's not into that. Although I feel springy, even quite thirsty. Things have changed. Addition does that. Although it's impossible to know whether it's addition or subtraction. Halifax does that. But there is no new language, nothing essentially different. My feet itch and the candy bar has made me hungrier. I can no longer hear an engine or see a blinking light.

Flagstaff spoke:

"Recall a situation in a crater south of here. A toy train was used to run around what was left of us and mechanize the circle. The train would stop and whoever was nearest would announce the station: Chattanooga, Mendocino, Little Rock, Fall River, Las Vegas, Seattle, Minneapolis, New Orleans, El Paso, Sioux City."

Halifax touched Flagstaff's arm. Flagstaff knocked Halifax's hand away. Halifax stood up and walked back to the spot where he had come from. He sat down, his back to Flagstaff and the stranger. The three bodies formed a triangle. The bushes were in front of Halifax, the statue behind Flagstaff and the trunk behind the stranger.

Halifax sits in an open space in an open land. He accepts neither what has come before nor what will come next. This must be my voice. The voice of Halifax. Behind me there are probably two men. We'll form a company or group and go from there. Halifax is not stagnating. He will keep the chill from his bones. He will gather together an occasion. I want to keep it open. Something always happens even if nothing happens. Halifax's voice has digested a part of the disintegrating whole. That isn't true but it has a certain sound, a specific ring to it. Halifax will establish a sound. With Omaha the sound was only half there. He kept slipping back to Memphis. He lacked authority. He lacked commitment. He labored over the simplest statement. He was never able to converse with Flagstaff; he never drew him out, never established a common area, a common goal, common information. I noticed all that and yet it happened. It has

a way of happening. As Halifax knows full well. But Omaha
was a casualty, failing as he did to recognize any necessity for
coming together with Flagstaff. I like the sound of that: Failing as he did to recognize any necessity. Halifax should mention that when last seen Flagstaff was holding the knife. Omaha
lost or dropped the knife. It was a final gesture, to let me know
just how incompetent he was. One must assume that Flagstaff
has the knife, gripped between his dying fingers. Nothing came
of Omaha's solipsism. Only the stingiest of complaints. Halifax must consider Flagstaff and the stranger together, in the
same breath, as if they occupy the same space. That is danger-
ous, of course, leaving me on the outside, facing the bushes.
There are two of them and one of me. That can be fixed. I can
turn around. But that would be too fast, too generous. I am
not traveling rapid transit. Not enough has happened for me to
turn and rush forth, bringing it all together. Halifax is nowhere
near being irresistible. He has my own shabby façade, my own
self-consciousness, my own compulsion to deal with the night,
to devour myself so that nothing finally will be left. Memphis
should have stayed on. I feel the scar of his separation. I should
never have abandoned him. His tortured pose had an end within
it. He would have consumed himself. This progression of false
names is impossible. There is no material for speculation. And I
have only time for speculation. The Lord help me to say something that doesn't echo what my ears took in. But I don't have
to digest all of this. Halifax will do that. Halifax will not give
me away, he is anonymous, not easily recognized. He will bring
the circle together... No good. Halifax is paralyzed. He can't
turn around for fear the knife might be on the ground behind
him and not poised to plunge into the back of his neck. How
did all this become so heavy? A third person will do that. Will
drive everyone into corners to talk to themselves. The common
focus, so shaky to begin with, splits and fractions off. And I was
nearly engrossed somewhere back there. Something, someone,
was holding my attention. It wasn't the fire, that didn't work,

and it wasn't the oak tree. I was never interested in the oak tree. Nor was I interesting in holding to my spot. That was Flagstaff's play. A pathetic manipulation to arrange the board for his own advantage. It was the engine. The sound of the engine stayed with me, even when it hasn't been present. I always hear the sound of the engine. The engine is part of every gesture, every word that squeezes through my tightened lips. Halifax is unable to share these thoughts. It doesn't matter. Flagstaff would put them down. There is no way of getting through, not without violence, a shared disaster. But is that not the case? That sounds like Omaha, the bitterness, the solitude, the futility. Now Halifax comes forth. He has different proposals.

Flagstaff spoke. The stranger answered.

"I would welcome wood to the fire. Even paper. The heat doesn't have a reach to it."

"I'm the addition to the fire and my feet are warm."

"That might not be the way to start an association. I walked too long and too far to watch the fire die."

"My feet happen to be next to the fire. I'm not taking up anyone's space. I'm not obliged to do anything."

"I've come in here and I've eaten here and I've slept here and I've moved around here. This space is exactly staked out."

"This is the fucking park. I got as much right to this can as you do."

Flagstaff has an audience. Or perhaps Halifax is the audience. He is most likely at their mercy, not being able to contribute. But perhaps they are at his mercy, not being able to acknowledge his presence. There is no mercy. The stranger's voice is youthful, with an edge to it. He hasn't walked far. The two voices don't complement each other.

Flagstaff sat cross-legged, staring at the ground in front of him. The stranger lay with his head on the trunk, his feet touching the garbage can. He had opened his eyes and was looking at Flagstaff. The fire had nearly died and the space between the oak tree and the statue was thicker, almost impenetrable. The lines and objects on the ground were invisible. Halifax sat with his back to the circle. The knife lay behind him. Overhead an engine droned. The three figures had difficulty breathing. The stranger sat up and took of his yellow rain slicker. He folded the rain slicker into a neat square and placed it on the trunk. Then he lay down with his head on the rain slicker.

Flagstaff spoke to the stranger, his eyes focused on the ground in front of him:

"We have to put it together. There are considerations."
"I gave up considerations."
"Do you have food?"
"Some."

Halifax heard a series of short steps behind him. The steps ceased. Flagstaff and the stranger sat and lay as before.

The space behind is my head. There is nothing more. What then is in front? Bushes. The action lies to the rear. Halifax should turn. It doesn't matter. The action is all around him. He can walk to the bushes or the fire. The stranger brought wetness into the area. Flagstaff and Halifax were dry. I can turn around; that wouldn't initiate a foray or endanger a beginning. There being a few spoils to grab. There is nothing behind and nothing in front. That's over my head. The space behind Halifax, around me, inside me, is Halifax's head, my mind. I suspect that. But hopefully this space and these distinctions will disintegrate and finally drop away and Halifax will walk out of here a free and single man.

Flagstaff crawled up behind Halifax and whispered to him:

"I was getting settled. You saw that. He has walked through ashes and mud. I noticed his boots. But that isn't the disruption. I asked him to get started with the fire. He refused. He has to know he can't mess around with what has been set up. There isn't that much time."

"It's like a slimy pool back there."

"My thought exactly. There's too much debris. We need a map, some kind of control."

Flagstaff picked up the knife that lay behind Halifax. He walked over to the garbage can and stuck the knife into the ground near the stranger's exposed foot. Kneeling, he groped for twigs and pieces of wood. He found two wooden slats from a charred crate. He put them into the garbage can. The stranger helped. Together they increased the fire. Then the stranger lay back on the yellow rain slicker. Flagstaff sat cross-legged, watching the fire. Halifax sat staring at the bushes. Overhead an engine droned and a blue light blinked.

I will turn around. Halifax needs to experience that vast garden behind me, where rubber bands exist next to crushed Dixie Cups. The bushes are soothing. There is no point of reference. There is something more, an empty stare. The bushes restore silence. I don't have to turn as long as Halifax keeps staring at the bushes. If I was to suddenly turn, Halifax would have to search for an object to focus on and that might not lead to anything. He might get stuck. If only he can avoid a contest. There is too much struggling, even though the competition has long ago been over. No one has handled Flagstaff. They became too involved. Memphis and Omaha considered him closely. It wasn't necessary. And now Halifax has lost his concentration. And I am no longer staring at the bushes.

Flagstaff whispered directly behind Halifax:

"Listen, Omaha, we need boundaries. No one keeps to their spot. We need everyone to keep to their spot."
"This is my spot."

Flagstaff waited several minutes and then whispered to Halifax:

"Says his name is Abilene. Says he doesn't recall or care where he came from or where he's going. Says that I'm foolish to come on the way I do. But then, I'm old. Says there is water back a quarter of a mile. Says we should choose who is to go for water and who is to go for wood."
"We'll think on that."
"Things are out of hand. You can't keep out of it forever. If we're going to establish some kind of last terminal, you should turn around."

Flagstaff returned to his original spot. The fire glowed softly. Abilene slept. Halifax stared toward the bushes. There was no sound, no movement of any kind. Flagstaff walked over to the garbage can. He bent over and removed the knife from the ground. He held the knife in his left hand and returned to his original spot. He fell twice but each time he managed to recover. When he arrived at his original spot, he executed a slow about-face and began to pace back and forth. Abilene opened his eyes and watched him.

What is it that I want? Halifax shouldn't answer that question. He can no longer see the bushes, only a density. These words bring it all down. Halifax has trouble surrendering himself to a vacant stare. Flagstaff's pacing doesn't help. That starts the flow of words. The necessity now is to fix on a particular.

Memphis and Omaha probably needed stories. Perhaps that is
what they were waiting for, unless they themselves were stories.
Halifax couldn't swallow the invention much less participate in
the drama. It's a definite loss but not one to linger over. Halifax
smiles. His whole face is possessed by an all-embracing smile.
If these words would run out and refuse to begin again then
something would happen. Although Halifax is not up to turning around. But I don't want my fade-out to be in front of the
bushes. I don't have the equipment to make a go of that. Flagstaff and Abilene must be ignoring me. I haven't contributed to
the evening. I have trouble distinguishing their differences much
less my own. Halifax doesn't pay attention, but distinctions pile
up and run over each other, freezing my smile. Halifax distrusts
emotion that comes directly from words. I have insisted on that.
But nevertheless I am holding something back. It's as if this lo-
calized hysteria results from not managing the space behind me
and not transcending the one in front of me. If Halifax and I
could get something together, back and forth, we could stay out
here and take it like it comes. But Halifax is heavier, more severe
than Omaha. I can sense that. And the complaint, the loss has
deepened and I am further along.

Flagstaff spoke to Abilene:

"The oak tree is one boundary. The statue will be the other.
East to west. Call it that. North will be the bushes. There are
bushes over where he's sitting. I'll be south. No, that's not right.
I'm in the middle between east and west. I'll be a halfway point.
We'll have to make a south."

After a long silence, Abilene replied:

"I want to let it happen quietly, like that man checking out the
bushes. I don't want to be bugged."

"We'll fall apart if everyone does that. We don't have much time. Besides, he's a loser."

"Passed a man coming in. He was sitting quietly near the swamp. Called himself Cincinnati. Didn't see any reason to come on in. Said he wanted to see it through where he was."

"You're not in to helping out."

"I'm tired. I can't go no farther. I helped with the fire."

"You can't tell what's out there or what will happen. Best not to know. If we don't put it together here it will fall apart."

"I don't directly know but I think it has already come apart."

Abilene shut his eyes. Flagstaff stared at the ground in front of him. The air was thicker, harder to breathe. Flagstaff grasped the knife and extended the line nearest him two feet toward Abilene. The gesture tired him.

It has just occurred to Halifax that he might be involved in the formation of a landmark.

Abilene slowly crossed his left leg over his right. Flagstaff crawled a few feet to the red cigarette package and recovered it. He crawled back to his original spot and placed the cigarette package in the small pile in front of him.

Flagstaff crawled up to Halifax and whispered directly behind him:

"Abilene will stay between the garbage can and the trunk. I think we can count on that. I'll stay halfway between the can and the statue. You stay where you are, within ten feet of the bushes."

Flagstaff crawled back to his original spot.

These last moments have been oblique. I'm not involved. Halifax can't hear the words spoken. Are they more interesting than the words thought? The balance is off. I should rush forth. I have only Halifax to lose. I should let everything rip. Halifax holds back. It all seems the same to him. But I haven't smelled or tasted anything. Although I have noticed gestures, the pathology of a walk. Flagstaff's walk, for instance, is stiff and brittle, as if his shinbones have been split. It is only his spirit. There has been no taste to hang on to. The candy bar was only substance. A mild chew. I could have passed time on each crunch. I might not be trying to break though. I might not know what that means. Halifax could be holding fast to a set of limitations. No one discusses motives, as if there might not be any. For instance: how to eliminate me, or each other. What gets it up. What keeps it down. Little fillers. We all know strategies exist. I prefer the engine, as a part of my breathing. Halifax holds me to that. I don't travel anywhere without the sound of the engine. Memphis and Omaha would never have embraced that. They could barely acknowledge the engine. Halifax is not aware of beginnings or endings. He's not attached to the progressions that so obviously affect me.

Halifax stared at the bushes. Flagstaff added to the objects that were forming a circle. Abilene slept. An engine throbbed overhead. Abilene's arms were spread out on the trunk. His legs were wide apart. Flagstaff's lips moved slowly, his tongue falling occasionally over his lower lip. Halifax's hands discovered a tuft of grass.

Halifax never knew there was grass. He was never aware if a place was soft or hard, if he approached it fast or slow. He discovered nine blades of grass. Each blade is autonomous. His fingers squeeze a tip. He grazes over the whole. I have my eyes closed. The blades are as long as my hand. Halifax eats the grass while I pick it, throwing it up in the air and letting it float. Halifax no longer needs the static shape of things to hold on, to know where I am. The simplest blade of grass leads to the most banal of speculations.

Halifax stared at the bushes. Flagstaff gathered the objects he had used to form a circle and threw them before him, like bones. Abilene opened and closed his eyes. The blocks of smashed cement that had once been a statue leaned forward, as if trying to form one image.

Flagstaff crawled up to Halifax and whispered directly behind him:

"He's coming around."

Flagstaff returned to his original spot. He sat cross-legged, staring at the objects before him. Abilene slept.

I've come this far without deliberation. Halifax addresses himself to no one. He recognizes no consequence to anything I say or do. He has relinquished all claims to any space I might need. Halifax was unable to distinguish whether Flagstaff spoke to Abilene or Abilene spoke to Flagstaff. In any case, they both spoke and they both answered:

"I can't manage the openers."
"Don't try."
"You understand. We have to move out."
"You've been involved in that."
"We're all involved in that."
"I'm not helping myself initiate an action."
"We have to establish a wider range. We have to have room to spread out."

"I don't."
"This is oppressive."
"You should split."
"That might happen."

I could force an action. I could stop this subversion. I could move on. Halifax has established authority. His emaciated back has become dominant. He suggests a lack of effort.

Flagstaff walked over to the garbage can and kicked it over with his foot. Sparks flew. Coals landed on Abilene. Abilene brushed the coals to the ground. Flagstaff kicked and maneuvered the can so that it fit over the narrow end of the trunk. Then he kicked coals under and around the trunk. He stepped out of the light and returned with moldy strips of newspaper. He placed the newspaper on top of the coals. Abilene sat down on the other side of the trunk and together they blew on the coals. They ignited the trunk. Flagstaff returned to his original spot. Abilene folded his yellow rain slicker on the ground, a few feet from the burning trunk. He lay down on one elbow and looked impassively at Flagstaff.

Flagstaff spoke, his eyes focused on an edge of the yellow rain slicker:

"There's plenty of material. I use what's around. But I don't know how to properly take the next step."
"It's a demented pilgrimage. Myself, I would never venture forth to tear down or build up, what's around. Not now. Not after what's happened."
"Water isn't here."
"We have earth, stone, wood, fire, but we don't have water."
"We'll have to get water."
"I'm too tired to go for water."
"Cincinnati should come in. He should come in with water."

If Halifax could make it with the bushes, I wouldn't follow what goes on behind me. As it is, I want to venture forth. I need a camouflage first, of course, to rest up a little, to grasp what's around. Everything is bound to reverse itself. The more voices, the more silence. A voice grows inside me, or the lack of a voice. A pressure. I can't keep staring. Halifax should do me in. While he can. I should prostrate myself before the bushes. Anything to avoid traveling to the next space.

Flagstaff crawled up to Halifax and whispered directly behind him:

"You've been elected to go for water. There's a swamp beyond the fire, about two hundred yards. You have to make a gesture if you're going to be with us. Abilene walked through the swamp on his way here. He calls it a children's pond but I'm telling you it's a swamp. Cincinnati sits somewhere out there. You can bring him in."

Flagstaff walked back to his original spot. He sat cross-legged, staring at the yellow rain slicker and then at the slow fire underneath the trunk.

Flagstaff goofed. No one is elected. He can't handle the pressure. He is no longer able to sit cross-legged, staring at the ground in front of him. He has become distracted. He can't face the night. He overreacts to everything. Halifax puts him down. That's good enough for me. Flagstaff is not about to make a trip. He will never leave this space. He probably knows that. Halifax and Abilene don't care whether they come and go. They never exactly arrived, so they can't become involved in departures. It's a definite task, to pick up the tin cup and wander two hundred yards beyond the trunk and fill the cup with water. To stand and look calmly ahead, perhaps at Cincinnati, to remember bearings, to drink and then refill the cup, to look back, to recheck bearings and then to start forth in the proper direction and know it is the way back. I wouldn't do it if I was Halifax. It would be madness.

Abilene spoke to Flagstaff:

"This must be a station or some kind of terminal."
"We haven't determined anything but it could be a disposal area or a site or a rendezvous. I don't know. Most likely some kind of bypass or recessed area."
"I'll match this space against any that comes along."
"Don't put me on."
"When we drink and get rested we should pack up and move on."

Flagstaff gathered the objects that were spread out in a half circle. Abilene watched. Behind Abilene the trunk was wrapped in flames. Flagstaff put the objects in his sack and sat down. He flipped the knife forward, so that it landed on the rain slicker. Abilene picked up the knife and held it in the palm of his hand. He stepped over the narrow end of the trunk and scratched a line toward Halifax. Abilene sat down and looked at Flagstaff. Flagstaff met his gaze and then stared at the ground in front of him.

I have used up all I have to say. That's Halifax speaking. We both want to use up all we have to say. Memphis had nothing to say. Omaha had little to say. The engine throbs on and off. There is just enough happening. The space behind me comes from everything I've learned or failed to learn. We all want to move out, to imprint an image on another space. But there has been nothing established. There has been no information. Thank god. We are saved an adventure

Flagstaff asked Abilene a series of questions:

"Do I seem emotionally flat?"

"Sure, why not."

"Did you come to this place in the same way you came to the last place?"

"No."

"Was it hard for you to leave the last place?"

"Yes."

"You must have separated yourself from sequences."

"I don't know what that means."

"Is it all or nothing with you?"

"Instead of being apart from a locale, we'll be within it. We'll be it."

"Are there still beautiful places around?"

"No. There isn't even conversation."

"Do you find it strange that you would be willing to sit still like this and not make a move, not take any kind of action?"

"I've forgotten about that. Otherwise it would be weird. But I'm into forgetting. That's one of my moves."

"Are you turned on to the colors and spaces between people?"

"Sure, why not."

"How do you reckon these questions?"

"I don't."

"Do you think?"

"No."

"Do you think we'll put it together?"

"No."

"What did you think of your last place?"

"I don't remember. I'm tired now. It's not necessary to go on with this."

Halifax can't distinguish their voices. They have become academic. They must be afraid. I don't mind that. It's a welcome abstraction. I know I'm going for water. Halifax can't turn around and he can't stare at the bushes. I have to walk straight through with a purpose in mind. Water will do.

Abilene appeared to be dozing. Flagstaff watched the trunk feed the fire while his hands emptied the sack. He let the objects lie without arrangement. The space had become smaller, more constricted. A long pain swept through Flagstaff's frame. He bent forward, blood dribbling from his mouth. His forehead touched the ground. He slowly raised himself. He tried to speak but no words came forth. A blue light blinked overhead. The flames rose a few inches and the air was thick with smoke.

It will be a beautiful walk to the lake. No doubt. I need a change, a small shift now that Halifax is strangling on his own spot. I can't move, after all. It is so peaceful here. There have been few threats and only occasional firing in the distance. But the area has grown too collective. We have been squeezed together after long runs. But I shall miss the voices more than the bushes. The sound was coming together, lower and lower, as if in accord with the engine around us. If I can just make it to Cincinnati. Perhaps we can return together. I can reassure him as we approach. Before the light uncovers us, we can separate and welcome the area from opposite sides, in case everything has changed… But now that I have decided to leave, I want to stay. Halifax is a staying man. He is involved with waiting out arrivals and departures. Perhaps it was Halifax that Memphis was pointing toward. To abandon a station after it has become grounded would negate the beginning. But the beginning has been destroyed. It's only these sentences that have to be forgotten. When Halifax was staring at the bushes, there was no information and he was no longer Halifax. Finding his name, he has to go for water in order to lose himself again.

Flagstaff stood on trembling legs and beckoned toward Abilene. He gestured for him to come closer, perhaps to listen, but Abilene closed his eyes. Flagstaff spread out his palms and patted the air before him. His ten fingers joined together in front of his eyes. They failed to hold and his hands dropped heavily to his sides. He stood motionless and then staggered and fell. He raised himself and sat cross-legged, staring at the fire.

I am moving out.

Halifax stood. His legs were stiff but his momentum determined a pivot toward the fire. The light made him close his eyes. He stepped forward, opening one eye, then the other. He walked toward Flagstaff. Abilene watched him. An engine droned overhead. Halifax stood before Flagstaff. He slowly picked up the crushed Dixie Cup, fashioning it to its original form with his fingers. He walked past Flagstaff, finding himself an equal distance from the smashed statue and the burning log. Abilene lay behind him now as he moved out of the circle of light. He walked slowly, looking neither to the right nor to the left. He reached the darkness. When he no longer knew where he was, Wichita sat down.

My language is not connected to an event, a Dixie Cup being the only object that holds me together. It is worse than when Memphis crawled in. I don't care to look around, having disappeared in all directions. Halifax didn't last long. He was gentle and ambivalent, strung out as he was on the outside line. The tension that held him apart from the action inside the circle gave him a posture, an inhibition that came close to privacy. Despite his silences, Halifax had presence, even character. He was a comedian… I feel too separated to go on, to bring events up to date, although Wichita is in the exact center of the country. Wichita is a flat and lonely place committed to the production of machines. I barely remember Wichita, having gone through just fast enough to steal a car.

Wichita sat on a deflated truck tire in the middle of an abandoned blacktop road. Flagstaff and Abilene were several yards behind him. The swamp sank off both sides of the road. Wichita's feet performed a series of shuffling maneuvers on the cracked tar. One foot would circle the other, then the other foot would swing around heel to toe. The air was very still. There was no sound, no light in front of him.

It is dark, there being no moon. Wichita is not particularly thirsty. He might be on a road, although I don't remember Flagstaff mentioning a road. How clear Flagstaff becomes in the darkness. He was much smaller than he first seemed. He might have been shot through the stomach, the way he kept bending over. He was babbling most of the time. Omaha stopped listening. Halifax never listened. It is a relief that Wichita never had to make a decision about Flagstaff. But then Wichita is detached from decisions, having been assigned a task. There is an arrogance connected to his relationship with the Dixie Cup, which he holds before him with both hands. I am tempted to crush the Dixie Cup, to start anew, to erase the direction I was pushed into so long ago. It isn't as if I've left valuables behind. It would be an expansive trip to freak out across the fields. I probably have one last run in me before I collapse into numbers. Wichita could run to Cincinnati, wherever that is. I know the circle is closing. I know the only way I can free myself from suffocation is to suffocate, to let my breath become theirs. I know that. But one last run won't hurt my chances.

Wichita stood up. Holding the Dixie Cup in one hand, he ran into the swamp. He entered up to his knees, the mud covering his brown suede shoes. He filled out the cup with his fingers.

Then he dipped it into the wet. He drank, holding the water in his mouth before he spit it out. He sank into the mud. A frog croaked. Overhead a blue light blinked twice. Wichita made no move, uttered no sound.

The water is foul and brackish. The taste still lingers in my mouth. It is a relief to hang in to a taste. I want to stand here tasting. I've forgotten about taste as I have about so many other senses. It's a pleasure to feel stagnation in my mouth. If I can just let it spread through the rest of my body. But even that passes, leaving my tongue hanging loosely over my front teeth.

Wichita turned and ran twenty steps to the road. He sat down on the tire. Then he stood and walked to the other side of the road. He tested the bank with a mud-caked shoe and advanced two steps. The ground swayed. He scratched his thigh, then moved on, stepping into plastic containers, broken bottles and rotting produce. Wichita's sense of smell had long since disintegrated, but he experienced dampness, a heaviness at the end of his nasal passages that slowed his walk, nearly buckling his knees. He moved on, his feet sucking into the soft fill. He broke into a stumbling trot. There were no stars, no lights to guide him, although a faint glow to his right could have been the fire half-surrounding Flagstaff and Abilene. He rested on a pile of eggshells and tin cans. He carefully flattened the Dixie Cup and put it into his pocket. Then he stooped and tore off the label from a can of sardines and put the label in his pocket. He ran but his breath failed and he was forced to walk. His left foot sank through a cardboard box, reappearing without the shoe. He turned and made his way back to where he thought he might have come from, his foot bleeding and his jacket and pants ripped. He entered a small clearing of sandy loam. An oil pump lay tilted on its side. A man slept with his head on the edge of the oil pump, a black fur coat covering him. Wichita sat down.

Leaning forward, he made an effort to speak but he nodded off. When he woke, the man was staring at him.

The man spoke:

"Did you find cans?"
"I got a label."
"There's food in some of the cans."
"I'm looking for water."
"I got tonic I found in a bottle. It ain't blessed with fizz but you're welcome to a taste."

The man took a bottle from underneath the overcoat and set it upright beside him. His face was round and dark. One side was heavily lined, the eye squinted shut and the mouth stretched down into a bitter exclamation. The other side of the face was smooth, the mouth a smiling arrow pointing toward a wide and staring green eye. Wichita poured a few inches of tonic water into the Dixie Cup. He drank it quickly and poured himself another shot, placing it on the ground before him.

Wichita forced himself to speak:

"Are you Cincinnati?"
"Can't exactly recall."

Wichita should go back. He has what he came for. A sip for all of us. Cincinnati isn't important. It was more the necessity of carrying something back that could be shared. Wichita could find a few cans and maybe a bottle of tonic water. There isn't that much time left. Wichita has the sense of being part of a continuum. He can't break the line. I know, of course, that there is no line but that, too, is crippling. Wichita, being a traveling man, needs a source. My sources have long since become irrelevant. But I resent having to go back. What would it take to keep Wichita on the move? He certainly knows how to move through space without attaching himself to local definitions. But he needs the limitations of a task. I should find an impossible quest for him. In any case, we're not fully sprung either way.

Wichita spoke:

"Which way you headed?"

"I'm going to catch it here. Don't hardly matter to me if I have company or not."

"We got a fire going. The space is cleared and smooth. A man could wait it out there in comfort. Only but two others at last count."

I should come back with someone. Abilene expects Cincinnati, although he won't know the difference. He's after a different kind of contribution. Another body and we would be protected on all sides. We could face the center, our backs to the outside, to the fire. It is that focus that Wichita strives for.

Wichita asked the stranger a question:

"How do they call you?"
"Been calling me Tacoma."
"Do you think you could see your way... Listen, come on back with me. I can manage the direction."

Tacoma didn't answer. Wichita sat down and prepared to wait. He crossed his legs and folded his arms. His foot had stopped bleeding but his head had begun to throb. He listened to the soft sounds of the garbage shifting in the dark. He could barely see Tacoma even though he sat ten feet from him. His fur coat blended in with the base of the broken oil pump. The drill bent downward and only the bottle of tonic water was fully visible. Wichita stared at the bottle.

Tacoma has something going for him; that is, if he's healthy enough underneath the fur coat. He might not have any legs. All I know is that he has one arm and a head. That would make it easier for me. I could move out quickly enough. I wouldn't have to convince him to come along, a situation Wichita seems committed to. Otherwise it will be hard, short of dragging him. The space here is natural and soft. It's not every day one comes across sandy loam. Food and drink are nearby. There are even a few rats to remind Wichita of animal life. Tacoma must have just crawled in. I doubt if he has been lying here for more than a week. He reminds me of Memphis: sullen, self-involved, paranoid. The dumb prick will have to be ramrodded into a standing position.

Wichita stood up and shouted:

"Drop your cocks and grab your socks."

There was no movement from Tacoma. Wichita sat down and resumed his former position. A blue light blinked overhead. He stared at the light. Because of his unnatural shout and the stiffness of his standing position, the space had grown smaller, the air colder. The piles of garbage outside the small area seemed to be moving closer. Wichita shut his eyes.

Tacoma spoke softly:

"No way you're going to get me to move."

Wichita has him now. Tacoma is waiting for me to convince him. If I throw a little heat his way he'll come. He's waiting it out, but the awareness of each light that passes overhead pins him to the ground. He'll come. Wichita has no choice but to see to that. The trouble with Wichita is that he is corny. This move toward transcending the self is not without its embarrassing moments. He has traveled too far, seen too many towns to be able to fully locate himself in any one moment.

Tacoma spoke:

"You might say something. I'm not in the habit of having a stranger stare at me. It blows my mind."

He wants a guarantee. But what is it that I have to promise for him to deposit his bones on another space? Wichita will never know. He will rely on silence. It is a cheap shot, but his silence is more complicated than most. He will wait Tacoma out. Either that or he will stand up and move on himself, forgetting to return.

Wichita stood up and walked around Tacoma, looking always to the outside. Tacoma followed him with his open eye. Wichita stopped and picked up the Dixie Cup. He didn't drink from it but continued his walk around Tacoma.

I never should have gone for water. It was a disaster. The relief to be away is too great. There is too much emotion. Wichita can't hold on any object. He's spinning here on the sandy loam. I blew it back there. It doesn't matter that the Dixie Cup is my return ticket. It will have to be different when I get back. Wichita has no choice but to return with Tacoma. To reenter alone will send me back to Memphis again, only at more of a disadvantage. Already I have forgotten the terrain back there. I can remember the fire clearly enough but none of the objects. I'm not sure where I was sitting or who was sitting in front of me.

Wichita sat down a foot away from Tacoma and spoke directly into his ear:

"The area is about forty feet. There are concrete blocks at one end and a burning log at the other. Flagstaff sits with his back to the concrete blocks and Abilene sits with his back to the burning log. An engine circles around. There is still one half a candy bar, possibly even more. The ground is rough but there are tufts of grass and a row of bushes on one side. The blue light overhead never gets in the way like it does here. I'm going to make it to the road and then find my way back."

Wichita stood up. Holding the Dixie Cup in front of him with one hand, he stepped backward.

Tacoma spoke:

"I'm coming too. You threw too many words at me. Take me too long to get back to where I was. But don't expect me to be grateful."

Wichita helped Tacoma stand. He had no clothes on underneath the fur coat and one leg was missing. Tacoma tried to hop but fell down. Wichita smoothed out the Dixie Cup and put the bottle of tonic water into a pocket of the fur coat. He helped Tacoma stand. Tacoma held on to Wichita's shoulder and managed to hop beside him. They left the clearing together. Tacoma fell again. Wichita helped him up. They managed another ten feet before Tacoma pitched forward. He sank into a brown pile of disintegrating lettuce and ripped paper plates. He lay still for a long moment, his open eye focused on Wichita's pant leg.

Tacoma finally spoke:

"I've gone too far. You might not figure it to look at me but

I was wiped out where I've been. No one getting through. I had to do several people in to get this far. The whole scene strangled, uptight. I can't be a part of any more last-minute schemes."

"Listen, Tacoma, I'm trying to forget about my own head. It's taken me too far so that there's not enough time to let you cash it in alone. I have to take you with me. You understand that. I got to have you to refer to."

"You must be some kind of fascist."

Wichita pulled him to his feet. Tacoma laughed with the downtown side of his mouth. They stumbled on, Tacoma throwing his full weight on Wichita, dragging his foot and wrapping both arms around his neck.

Wichita can't go on. I have to go on. Wichita is possessed. He needs the weight of Tacoma to give him focus, to make him remember that he has chosen to go back. He feels it a rare luxury to have his windpipe nearly crushed by a complaining cripple. His own foot bleeds. I can't talk to Tacoma, that's the pain. I can't offer explanations. My own information reaches me too slowly. But my fear of intimacy binds me to him. I can never leave him. I don't listen to him. I reply to someone else, some other voice. I don't know where I am. But Wichita will drag us both through.

Three rusted and broken iceboxes blocked their way. Wichita dropped Tacoma to the ground and leaned against an icebox that lay with its insides exposed to the sky. Tacoma dragged himself along the ground to an upright icebox. He managed to open the door. He crawled in, the door swinging shut except for his protruding leg. He rocked back and forth, tipping the icebox over. He lay inside the box with his bare foot exposed to the elements. Wichita crawled inside his own box. It wasn't big enough for him and his feet dangled outside. He stared at a blue light blinking above him. It was quieter inside the box. Nothing moved. His foot throbbed. He closed his eyes, then spoke:

"We'll take ten minutes here. Enough to get it together. Then we're moving out."

"Not me. I feel good inside this hole. I got my fur in here and solid protection. I'm warm for the first time in years. It's only my foot that's left out but it don't feel anything anyway."

Wichita might not be able to get out. If it was Memphis or Omaha, even Halifax, this would be a stopper. But Wichita can make it. He has to make it. He's beginning to nod off. He can't afford to do that. He's lost the thread enough as it is. There is no guilt inside here, no necessity, less fear. There is the metallic skin of the icebox. I am finally well wrapped. I might have to give up on Tacoma. If I pulled his foot it would probably come off. Wichita will have to make a deal for the tonic bottle. That is, if it's not broken. I'll give myself a few more minutes. The comfort is seductive. This moving around has broken me completely, even if it is the only way to reinforce the circle. Wichita had to move out in order to come back. The scratched lines had no strength. They were too easy to erase or step over. If we can make them solid enough we can encounter the last breath there. It will come soon enough. But song will pour from such a last stand. And Wichita will conduct the final choir, a vision that makes it easier to dispense with Tacoma.

Wichita spoke from within the icebox:

"Let's make a deal. I'll let you alone and you give me the tonic bottle."

"I want your jacket and your Dixie Cup half filled with tonic. I got to have me a pillow and some slosh to pour between my lips as I fade. I'm on the way out."

"I'll give you the Dixie Cup. I want the jacket. It's ripped anyway."

"You got some pair of balls. Next you'll be working for my coat. Then you'll want my foot, then this coffin here, then my very bones."

"I'll settle for the tonic bottle. You can have the jacket."

"Done."

Wichita has to keep moving or he'll slide back to Memphis. How Memphis would have leaped at the chance to lay up in an icebox. If we could fill the other box with someone, it might be possible to stay, although Tacoma has slipped badly. Someone would have to be waiting in the wings to replace him. Why not stay on? It is unnatural not to. Wichita insists. When he mentions the group gathered over yonder, when he refers to the collective "we," I am thrilled and terrified. He must still think he is part of the general area.

Tacoma spoke:

"Tell me the truth. When you leave me here it will give you a lift, right? It'll make you swell out a little, give some juice to your bones to know I'm staying out and you're going in."

"That's right."

"Well let me tell you something. You won't get no more of that kind of mileage from me. As far as I'm concerned you never happened."

Tacoma opened his door. Wichita lay with his hands underneath his head, staring at the darkness above. His elbows touched the sides of the icebox. There was no sound, no light.

Tacoma spoke:

"I'll tell you something else. There's someone inside that other icebox, someone trying to get out."

Perhaps Cincinnati has crawled in beside us. Wichita could take him back with him, although the presence of another body would weight the area. I might not be able to move. Especially if Cincinnati is unusually together. We would no longer be a small annex joined to the main force. We would be a separate planet with an orbit all our own. It is too late for all that. I will have to stay. Flagstaff and Abilene would become our extension; they will have to crawl in with us.

Wichita raised himself out of his icebox. He sat on the edge, peering about him. He could see directly into the third icebox which had a large hole in its side. It was empty.

Wichita spoke softly to Tacoma:

"Someone is in there. I'm coming over. Hand me the bottle."

He walked over to Tacoma's icebox and lifted the door off his battered leg. Tacoma's open and smiling side raised itself up at him and then turned to expose the downward pull, as if gravity had nailed him forever. Tacoma handed him the bottle and Wichita dropped in the jacket. As Wichita walked away, Tacoma said:

"Sure did talk to you."

Wichita replied from behind a hill of flattened crates:

"I saw you."

Wichita sat down on a dead motor. He removed the Dixie Cup from his pocket and filled it out. Then he poured himself a small drink from the bottle. A rat sniffed his bleeding ankle and moved slowly on. Wichita wore only a blue tee shirt now that his jacket was gone. He shivered and flapped his arms around his shoulders. He walked on, picking his way around broken glass and smashed metal. He carried the bottle before him in both hands. A blue light blinked twice. In the far distance an engine started and choked to a stop. Wichita reached the road and lay down, his arms and legs spread-eagled about him, his head rolling to one side.

At least the surface is hard. The pebbles that grind into my back are a relief. Wichita is always seeking relief. The need comes from his obsession with goals. He tries to leave too much behind. He is not boring enough. Memphis, Omaha and Halifax were all reliably dull. And so they never transgressed their space. Wichita might have blown the whole progression through his effort to unite the fragments. What bullshit. It's only one night he's playing with, even if that night might be terminal. He can either accept the dawn, the light or struggle to hold back, to express one last objection. We turn too slowly for him, he must create signals and signs. He must reach out and attach himself to the gesture. I fear Wichita. His momentum might turn us over.

Wichita stood. He looked up and down the road. Then he walked to the edge and sat down, his bare foot in the swamp. The ooze formed to his ankle. He closed his eyes. His breathing became slower. The sweat on his forehead dried. He stood again and moved back to the center of the road. He walked to where the road faded and ended. He sat down on the dry earth, setting the bottle in front of him. He stared at the top of the bottle, then the neck, then the body. He closed his eyes. He listened to deep breaths. They were not his own. He opened his eyes. There was a shape twenty feet to the front and slightly to the right of him. He waited until the shape became clearer. It was a rock, then a large potato, then a package of bent cigarettes. The shape emerged as a small figure sitting in a broken armchair.

Is this a tollgate? Does this mark the end of the road? We sit facing each other. I can't see whether it's a man or a woman. There is a large gray felt hat, a loose blue and white football jersey with the number 32. Baggy Army or bus driver's pants. Orange socks and sneakers. I can't distinguish the features, although the colors advance toward me. I need a drink but Wichita refuses to squander the fluid. It's a drag having him around. The flats are crowded; refugees must be constantly pouring in. Perhaps the figure is long deceased, having been propped up in the chair for a number of years.

The figure held up a hand and performed an awkward version of the Hand Jive. Wichita copied the gestures: he slapped both hands twice on his knees. Then he raised his hands chest high, spreading the fingers apart and holding the left hand above and parallel to the right hand. He slid the left hand over the right hand and then reversed the process. He pounded his left fist twice on his right fist, followed by his right fist on his left fist. He touched his left elbow twice with his right hand, then his right elbow twice with his left hand. The figure's hands began to move faster and faster until they lost control and broke out into a series of scratches. Both ears were scratched, then the left shoulder and the legs. The figure stooped and wrapped both arms around its legs and held on. It swayed back and forth and finally stopped. The figure stayed in that position. Finally it raised its arms, crossing them over the chest.

The figure spoke:

"I watched you sprint past. Figured I'd wait you out. No sense hailing a man bent on coming or going."

Wichita didn't answer. There was only the figure in the armchair and the orange socks.

The figure spoke:

"Trenton passed. Wanted me to come in with him. Wouldn't consider it. He didn't know of a location. Not that anyone does… I didn't like his reasons for wanting to settle down. He was too frantic. He kept falling down. I think he had lost an arm."

Wichita answered:

"We must pull the area together. Tacoma wouldn't come. He couldn't handle the language part. But we have to stand up and count each other. There isn't time for emotional theatrics."

Wichita can't keep his eyes away from the orange socks. Perhaps it's because the voice in front of me has no high or low register. It sinks into a monotone. I can't distinguish the sex. It doesn't figure for a cunt to be trying to locate herself out here. Not that they aren't around. But they're not known to drift after an apocalypse, preferring to hang on to whatever nest they may be into. That's Wichita's opinion but it's more like the voice of Memphis: self-involved, whispering, frozen. But how old are we all, anyway? It doesn't matter anymore. There is not enough time to consider the age of animals or objects. It all exists out front. So the camp must be near. I couldn't consider it if it was a day's walk. Wichita must have gone in the right direction. I could run a zigzag course right by the armchair and dive in. But Wichita can't move. Perhaps I'm afraid of going in alone. It won't be the same space. I'll need help. Wichita is determined enough, involved as he is in a particular set of moves. Adventure doesn't turn him off. But he'll have to allow for me. He'll have to carry me, complaining all the way. I'm not as attached to him as when he moved out for water. He was open then, curious and even vulnerable. Accomplishment gives him distance, an alien sort of poise considering the situation. He's too earnest, too unaware of another's needs, let alone existence. If only Halifax was sitting here, nodding toward his ankles. He could certainly handle the bottle and the orange socks, even the nightmare in the armchair. He would stare his way through with his own system of blinders and one-way responses. Memphis and Omaha would have been lost, of course, unable to cope with such ambiguous barriers. I am stalling. I've known it for a while. It's because Wichita is moving too fast. He has lost his tolerance for reminders, for the masochism of uncontrolled pauses. I want to slow down. But Wichita doesn't see the need for maps and rest stops at this late date. It's definitely a double bind. I would rather forget about time, rapping myself into oblivion if need be. He wills himself to transcend it. He believes in affirmative gestures. I don't believe. I need the fire and a soft rag for a pillow. No stomping as the breath fails, just a complaint sinking into silence. Wichita is involved with signs and monuments. He's even holding on to his name. Poor leader. Perhaps he has no fear of reentry, believing in it as he does. I'm paralyzed. Have I journeyed so far to be stopped by a crippled armchair and a pair of orange socks?

The figure spoke:

"Call me Cincinnati. I moved in a while ago. You might remember passing me on the way out. I want to get people arranged around the armchair. I can be the focus. It will help to pass the time."

The situation is not without its outlandish charm. Two adversaries facing each other, waiting it out with no weapons in sight. There will have to be some kind of agreement. If only Wichita could distinguish Cincinnati's features. They might give him a clue, not that anyone is in to clues these days. The whole scene is regressive. The language that has gone back and forth is no help, except for the already known fact that it has all been spoken before in different times, different places. I hope Wichita tries to fake left and go right. I hope he is hip enough to avoid the whole issue as I am trying to do.

Wichita sat cross-legged in a field of ragweed and occasional patches of rye. The space between him and Cincinnati was empty of growth so that the effect was that of a planned path leading up to the armchair. Wichita lay down, leaning on one elbow. He used the top of the bottle as if it was the sight of a rifle and stared into the middle of Cincinnati. His foot had stopped bleeding but it had begun to itch. He made no effort to scratch it.

Cincinnati spoke:

"Mister, I am in a swapping mood. I want your bottle and everything in your left trouser pocket."

Wichita regarded Cincinnati without expression. At no time did he appear hurried. He answered softly, keeping his eye focused on the middle of Cincinnati:

"I usually do a cash-on-the-barrel business. What have you got?"
"Orange socks. They'll stand cleaning but they only got two or three small holes. I'll throw in a few buttons and the right front leg of the armchair. It could make decent kindling."
"No deal."

Wichita fingers the bottle coldly, almost casually. He holds his ground as though it were of no importance. I have to hand it to him. He seems calm and sure of himself. Oh god, it is not a tonic bottle. The bottle is green and there is a strip of label on the lower half. It is a ginger ale bottle. I have been conned.

Cincinnati spoke:

"We can only get through this together. You need me to un-plug the energy. There's a lot of joy and horniness around here if you know how to let it happen."

Wichita sat up. He picked up the ginger ale bottle and rubbed it in his hands. He spoke with his eyes looking into the bottle:
"I don't want to brace you. I might have to move around you. I don't know what it will take to make you come on in."
"It will take more than you have to give. I'm comfortable enough."

Wichita stood up and stepped forward three paces. He held the bottle tightly against his chest with his left hand. His right hand scratched the top of his head. He slowly lifted the bottle and drank a small sip of dead ginger ale. At no time did he look away from Cincinnati. He placed the bottle on the ground before him and retreated three paces. He sat down and crossed his legs and began to scratch his neck and chest with both hands.

I need to walk some warmth into my feet. That might be the most important and sensible thing I can do. I'm played out. These maneuverings are too much to follow. Some other part of me will have to manage. Wichita obviously needs an activity to seduce either himself or Cincinnati. Or perhaps both. It is bet-ter if he does it without interpretation, there being no structure with which to refer to. It's not as if anyone is in touch with his sources. Motives are hard to come by when the issues have dis-integrated. For Wichita to get these flats together, he's going to have to come up with some heavy moves.

Wichita stood, still looking toward Cincinnati. His hands had stopped scratching and hung limply by his side. He stepped sideways five paces. He stood at the edge of the field of ragweed so that now there was a diagonal line between him and Cincinnati. Overhead a blue light blinked twice. Somewhere beyond the field of ragweed an engine droned. The ragweed grew as high as his stomach, with a few stalks tall enough to be in his line of vision if he were to look that way. He shifted his gaze from Cincinnati to the bottle. He stared at the bottle and then slowly followed the ground to a tuft of grass near his feet. Leaning next to the tuft of grass were three small cigarette butts. A foot away a scrap of yellow paper lay curled next to a broken plate. Wichita sat down. He took the Dixie Cup from his pocket and laid it flat on the ground. Then he reached forward and gathered in the cigarette butts, the scrap of yellow paper and the broken plate. He unfolded the yellow paper. On the paper were the words PROMISED FOR FRIDAY and, in smaller letters, Printed in U.S.A.

I have to make a choice. Either Wichita stops messing around and leaves Cincinnati and makes it back to where he started from or he stays and deals directly with the problem at hand. If he stays he won't be able to handle Cincinnati. There will have to be a change. Wichita does seem to have a plan in mind but if put into effect it would contradict his original purpose. He has already separated himself from the bottle. Wichita has been a strong attachment. He has led me away from something although I'm not quite sure what it was. But my sense of complaint has grown lately and it has strengthened the already unbearable sound of my voice. I'm not sure if I can forget anymore with him. It's true, since Wichita came on the scene, Memphis, Omaha and Halifax have receded. In fact, even the circle has grown dimmer. Flagstaff and Abilene no longer exist. They have their pull, to be sure, but I have been able to pull back. But I can't get through the night if I don't believe that at some point I'm going to return. It was Wichita's strong sense of direction that made it possible to leave. I knew he would get back. But that same strength is involved with some weird competition with Cincinnati. He might blow the whole thing.

Cincinnati spoke:

"You're not holding to a course. You're drifting. I'm pinned to this chair. I'm not complaining. I want to point that out. I can no longer travel through. I'm sitting in a soft chair unable to watch what is in front of me. I can't see. I can't hear. And yet I can see, I can hear. It's too much of a stretch to have you come up the path. I don't want to get into paths. Don't trade with me. Don't offer me water. Don't stay. I'm no longer inclusive. I can barely breathe."

"You can look at the bottle, then swing over to the plate. If you can manage that you can work over to the yellow paper."

"There is no problem, so there is no solution."

Duluth stepped cautiously into the ragweed. He moved slowly. Three feet into the ragweed he sank to his knees. He tried to smell the earth and was able to detect a faint musky odor. He licked the earth with his tongue. He surrounded a thin stalk of ragweed with five fingers and moved his hand up and down as if he was gently jerking off the stalk. He broke off a stalk and chewed it. It was very dark and he could see nothing around him except the ragweed. Above him an engine droned. He crawled back to the path and peered at Cincinnati and then at the bottle and the Dixie Cup and yellow paper. Nothing had changed. He reached out with one hand and removed the Dixie Cup, putting it in his left trouser pocket. Then he crawled back to where he had smelled the earth.

It was important for Duluth to leave a cairn both for direction and for Wichita. Wichita could have gone farther but his energy was becoming too frantic, too obsessive and the split was too wide. He was riding too much of a straight line. The separation is difficult because Wichita knew how to move but Duluth is a calm and deeply located place. The earth figures heavily around Duluth and the prairie rolls unbroken and unopposed through the Mississippi valley. There are no trees as now there are no trees. Duluth possesses quiet efficiency and will know how to engage Cincinnati without opposing him. Wichita was becoming competitive, as if he knew what the night held for him. It was a drag. His rigidity produced too much introspection. Duluth is more expansive. He's able to lift an object without rejecting its intimacy. He won't polarize voices; they will melt together more and distinctions of use and proportion will become less important. No, Wichita had to go. He was too earnest.

Duluth crawled forward, moving parallel now to the path. He kept his head low, as if searching for something on the ground. He was particular about his direction and the placement of his hands and legs as he crawled on. Every three or four feet he would stop. There was no sound, no movement save his own rustling passage through the ragweed. He stopped and pulled himself up to a sitting position. He crossed his legs and breathed evenly in and out.

Cincinnati spoke:

"I know you're out there. I can hear you. I can hear you moving through. Others have moved through. Trenton, Tacoma and Abilene have passed. No need to crawl. You can stand up and walk. What's your name? It's not like a man to pass through and not leave his name. That's not the kind of a station this is. It's not as isolated here as you might believe. I chose to be here. I could have gone in with Abilene."

Duluth crawled forward. He crawled over a bedspring and a broken sled. He passed a pile of cans and a smashed supermarket cart. The ragweed had thinned out and grew now in clusters. The earth had become rocky and cluttered with piles of rubbish.

Cincinnati spoke:

"I can still hear you. It's not anyone else. I came crawling in too, awhile ago. Well, fuck you. I know where you sit. I can see through the flames. There's too much heat. I could shed some clothes. Mary used to do that for me. I would lie down and she would undress me. Oh sure, I remember all that. Who are you talking to? What makes you think you can come in here and pull a stunt like that? I told you that if you hang out here you'll get it sooner or later. I told you. Didn't I tell you? I told you. Well, it's not going to happen. They've been saying it was going to happen but I'm telling you it's not."

Duluth crawled on. He was behind Cincinnati now and coming up on the other side. He was crawling at a steady pace, only stopping when he encountered a large obstacle and then he would crawl around. Above him a blue light blinked twice. There was no sound, no other movement in the ragweed. He passed Cincinnati and kept on crawling, moving in toward the path, as if he was completing a circle. When he reached the path he stood up and walked to the ginger ale bottle. He picked up the bottle and stepped three paces toward Cincinnati. He held the bottle tightly against his chest with his left hand. His right hand scratched the top of his head. He slowly lifted the bottle and drank a small sip of the dead ginger ale. Then he placed the bottle on the ground before him and retreated three paces. He sat down and crossed his legs and began to scratch his neck and chest with both hands.

Duluth is tightly organized but he's taking his time. He seems to feel it worthwhile to freak out the area. I'll hang in for a while. His movements are tightly controlled. That will become a problem, but for now it minimizes my sense of loss. I feel grief. I can't shake it. What, for instance, has happened to the turtle? I need lines around me, an established space with people moving through. I can't begin again. If only it were a spiral with a greater and greater focus. That is how it is supposed to move. It never does. There is no such thing as an interruption. I know Cincinnati is receiving too much attention. That the proportion is tilted. Although Duluth seems to know that proportion is an unnecessary invention. The first person is driving my nose closer and closer to my own asshole. We have to hold hands and not fear the releases. I am beginning to distinguish Cincinnati's features. His face is white. It might be covered with makeup or perhaps bandages.

Duluth stood, still looking toward Cincinnati. His hands had stopped scratching and hung limply at his side. He stepped sideways five paces. He stood at the field of ragweed so that now there was a diagonal line between him and Cincinnati. He shifted his gaze from Cincinnati to the bottle. He stared at the bottle and then slowly followed the ground to the cairn. Then he stared again at the bottle and slowly followed the ground to Cincinnati's orange socks and into the middle of Cincinnati. He looked into the middle of Cincinnati for several minutes. Then his eyes slowly retraced their passage, from the orange socks, to the bottle, to the cairn. After he had stared at the cairn, he stepped cautiously into the ragweed.

Cincinnati spoke:

"Get back. Get back. Come on back here. You're crawling farther away. I'm going to tell you. I've seen lots of people walk.

Is this some kind of full-court press? No, no. I'm coming closer. I never looked above. Colors there aren't. You can have the
socks. They're orange, you know. I don't know what color you're
moving through. Orange, red, green. What does it matter? I recall, no, I don't do that. Get back. I'm calling for Abilene. He set
this up. Abilene, get back."

Duluth crawled through the ragweed. He cut a wider circle
now but it will be closed off at the top. The circle will be oblong,
like the rock on top of the cairn. Duluth crawled at the same
steady pace, stopping every three or four feet, as if to listen. But
there was no sound, no movement through the ragweed save his
own rustling passage. The sky was lighter, either from a fire in
the distance or from a first hint of dawn. The ground was moist.
Duluth crawled around an oil can and over a hubcap. He faced a
smashed car. The tires were gone, the hood was caved in and the
windows were smashed. It was a blue four-door sedan. Duluth
crawled into the back seat and shut his eyes.

I didn't notice the make of the car. I don't need that. This is
just a small layover, a sidetrack. Duluth is not into images. He's
trying to cut that down. Duluth doesn't want any adventures
or sudden flashes. If Duluth has to flash, it will be on his own
emptiness. The night has been too stuffed, too fanciful. I had
thought Wichita was going to go straight out for water and then
straight back. He forgot or overran himself and then became
involved in tactics. Duluth has inherited all that but he might be
able to bring it more together if he is able to forget the source.
He's moving well, not getting trapped between sound and image. He's going straight through. Soon he will be able to take his
course for granted and his breath will even out. There are no
surprises in Duluth. It is a solid cornhusking place where questions are never asked. There is a foot hanging over the seat. The
foot is inside a black and torn basketball sneaker. The shoelaces

are untied. I'm not going to look. The foot hasn't moved. Perhaps it's only attached to a leg. I don't want to know. Duluth has most of his eyes closed. He's not going to get into it. He can hear no breathing, no moving around. If he stays cool he won't find anything out. There is enough to forget without this foot in his face. How many feet have trampled through this night? That is the kind of question that will get you in trouble, the kind Duluth passes over without emotion, without consideration. Wichita forgot about the necessities of negation. His map was simple enough even if it was connected to a purpose. But he flipped once he found himself off course. He forgot to concentrate on the most minimal of gestures. His signs became confused and he tried to direct traffic toward himself rather than letting it flow by. Duluth would prefer not to know about the traffic staggering through. That is not his concern. It is all directed at Cincinnati and with the problem of forgetting Cincinnati as he draws closer. I have to remember how to forget where Duluth is. So that he can go on. So that it will be possible to return. So that the dawn won't find us too excessive. So that we can start out again.

Duluth lay in the back seat with his hands behind his head, his eyes mostly closed. The foot with the black basketball sneaker hung over the seat a few inches from his head. The car had been blackened from fire and the upholstery burned so that Duluth lay on the twisted springs of the seat. The car still smelled of its own destruction. There was no sound inside or outside.

I can't afford to make a distinction about being inside a space. Duluth would be lost now if he surrounded the car with compulsions. I would never leave. It is too intimate here, too affective. There is too much poetry in the blackened colors and corroded smells. There would be too much expansion outside to think of. There is too much of value in here, too much magnified. There is not enough time to sink into that. Duluth would contain the outside because that is all there is. Of course, it is the same, we are surrounded even so, but neither Duluth nor I have time to figure that kind of unlimited strain. It is too remote and not remote enough. There is change here, but the innovation is impossible. Thank god there are no mirrors hanging around. I don't need to look into Duluth's moist eyes. Neither of us knows if we are moving toward the center or escaping. It is not important to know, only that we are moving, that the end doesn't find us too pinned to the end. No, these boundaries are definitely too comfortable. One could settle in here, to this openness. Outside one can move around; it is, after all, closed out there. So this is not a shelter, rather the reverse, a vastness that Duluth will never be able to handle.

Cincinnati spoke but Duluth was unable to distinguish the words.

Duluth crawled out of the car. He sat for a while, leaning against the bent door, to catch his breath after the exertion inside. Then he crawled on. He was behind Cincinnati now and coming up on the other side. He was crawling at a steady pace, only stopping when he encountered a large obstacle and then he would crawl around. Above him a blue light blinked twice. There was no sound, no other movement in the ragweed. He passed Cincinnati but kept on crawling, moving in toward the path. When he reached the path, he stood up and walked over to the ginger ale bottle. He picked up the bottle. Holding it tightly against his chest with his left hand, he stepped three paces toward Cincinnati. He slowly lifted the bottle and drank a small sip of dead ginger ale. Then he placed the bottle on the ground before him and retreated three paces. He sat down and crossed his legs and began to scratch his neck and chest with both hands.

Cincinnati's features are heavily made up with cosmetics. His face is broad, with wide-apart black eyes, a small pug nose and a large even mouth. The cheeks are round, the forehead small. He looks in my direction but his gaze is to the side. We must be ten feet apart now, perhaps slightly closer. I can almost hear his breathing. If he doesn't make a sudden move, Duluth will have him. His eyes look glazed, beyond the point of confusion. There is less effort now, the repetitions are dependable, as if there is beginning to be some kind of consistency between sound and image. Too much has already happened, of course, to set up any kind of channel. But perhaps he can be swept up in passing.

Cincinnati spoke in a whisper:

"I can feel the squeeze, if that's what you want to know. I can feel you coming in. I can even see your ugly face. You might be making it better. I can't decide. But I'm still pinned. I'm sucking you in or you're sucking me in. Your tracks are too spaced. You're not together enough. No, no, you're floating. I might have you. If you don't make a sudden move. You look ready to be taken. You look like you've been out there too long. None of those other places worked. Tell me the truth. All that shifting and crossing and recrossing and digging in and moving out and traveling through and getting across and resting up. It doesn't work."

Duluth stood, still looking at Cincinnati. His hands had stopped scratching and hung limply down. He stepped sideways five paces. He stood at the field of ragweed so that now there was a diagonal line between him and Cincinnati. Half turning, he shifted his gaze from Cincinnati to the bottle. He stared again at the bottle and slowly followed the ground to Cincinnati's orange socks and so on into the middle of Cincinnati. He stared at the number 32. Then, his head turning, his eyes retraced their passage, from the orange socks, to the bottle, to the cairn. He looked back at Cincinnati. His fingers were performing part of the Hand Jive. He pounded his left fist twice on his right fist, followed by his right fist on his left fist. He touched his left elbow twice with his right hand. Duluth followed the gestures. Cincinnati's hands lost control, waving in front of them as if to ward off a collision. Duluth stepped cautiously into the ragweed.

Cincinnati called after him:

"Best you swing it around faster this time. You've rocked me. You ought to give something. Not right to get that close without making it legal. Give something to hold in my hand. Rock me, baby. I'm stamping my foot. Can you hear that? Listen to that. One two three four five six, that's numbers. You know numbers? You're counting out a step. I know that. I know what you're doing. I can hear you."

I am so tired and yet so locked into this circle. But Duluth has managed to forget more than I thought he was capable of. He has transcended his own goodwill and now moves automatically, without thought, without plan. He is no longer aware of how long it takes to swing around Cincinnati, no longer aware that he joins himself every time he steps cautiously into the ragweed. I feel smoother, less distracted and more vulnerable, more open to the profane silence around me. But no matter what I think, Duluth will crawl on. He will crawl on until he drops or he moves through his own motions. I am not attached to Duluth and he is not attached to me. I am not concentrating as much as being concentrated upon. Perhaps this prepares me for the murder of my own solutions.

Cincinnati spoke:

"I took off my orange socks, you stupid fuck, and I threw them out in front of me. But I'm putting my sneakers back on. How do you like that? I said what? What?"

Duluth crawled on. He crawled past the car but only looked briefly at the fender. He was behind Cincinnati now and coming up on the other side. The air was heavy and smelled of burnt rubber. Duluth's eyes were bloodshot and red-rimmed, his head bent to the ground, his teeth biting into his lower lip. His knee pressed against a bar of soap. He stopped and sat cross-legged, folding and unfolding his arms against his chest. He picked up the blue cube of soap and pressed his thumb and forefinger into it. The soap had hardly been used. He smelled the soap and rubbed it against his cheek. He licked it with his tongue and took a small bite from it. Then he put the soap in his left trouser pocket and crawled on. Parallel with Cincinnati, he stopped again. Sitting cross-legged, he breathed in and out.

Cincinnati spoke:

"That is what I'm going to do. Three to the right and then four to the left. Gather it in. Now the count: seven, eight, nine. I'm still scared shitless. Yes, but I was thirsty. Never mind. These over there and now this. Like this. Better, much better. Sure I'm stiff. Rigor mortis is not exactly… that will do. That's an arrangement. The point is to keep busy. It's still dark but you never know how long that will last."

Duluth crawled on, moving in toward the path. He crawled slowly. One knee was bleeding and both hands were scratched and raw. He fell forward and lay motionless on the ground. His eyes stared at a black comb and the iron head of a hammer. Four of the comb's teeth were left and they were spaced far apart. Three stalks of ragweed grew between the hammer head and the comb. There were no insects along the ground. Duluth listened to an engine overhead. It was darker along the ground. He curled his legs up into his stomach and put his hands underneath his head.

I have no thoughts. I see everything before me. I hear everything around me. I smell as much as I can smell. When I move that is when I will move.

Cincinnati spoke:

"That's it for now. No more addresses. You called it. I'll throw in a few buttons. I won't have time to know how ruined I am. They won't catch me on the nod. I'm moving in. Never mind the map. The terrain doesn't matter. You take what you can't get. That's it. I'm cooking now. It doesn't matter if it's twenty, thirty or forty."

Duluth raised himself up. He kneeled with his head on the ground. Then he raised his head, shaking it back and forth. He slowly crawled forward. When he reached the path he stood up. He looked for the ginger ale bottle. It wasn't where he had last left it. He took two steps forward. Cincinnati wasn't in the broken armchair. He stepped forward again, facing the armchair. He was twenty feet away. He took another step. He looked neither to the right nor to the left. The armchair was dark blue with the covering ripped and two springs popping out of the seat. The missing back leg caused the armchair to tilt to the left as if wounded. Duluth stared into the inside of the armchair and took two steps. There was no sound, no movement around him. He took another step. Two orange socks lay in front of the armchair. He stared at them and then forced his gaze into the pit of the armchair again. He sat ten feet away. He heard a rustling behind him but was unable to consider it. His eyes lost their focus and he closed them. He stood still and tried to breathe evenly. Then he took two more steps. His entire body ached. The center of the armchair had grown warm and there was moisture on his upper lip and forehead. He was two feet away. The orange socks blocked his path. They were curled in on themselves as if trying to escape his gaze. He stepped on them. Then he took another step and sat down. When he opened his eyes Cincinnati was staring at him. He was sitting next to the ragweed in back of the cairn. Cincinnati looked at Duluth and took a long sip from the ginger ale bottle.

I'm pinned. I have come back on myself. Duluth thought, well, who knows what Duluth thought. It wasn't anything as banal as freeing Cincinnati. It couldn't have been from my own loneliness. It might have been an extension of Wichita's trip, trying to get someone to go back with him. It doesn't matter. I'm pinned. I can't move my back. I'm sunk in too deep. My arms lie on the rests the chair provides as if this will be their final posture. But I can't be totaled here. There must be a change somewhere. Duluth's endurance was a shuck. He was in to something totally different than he promised. Have I been led back to Halifax? Has the frontal stare of Halifax been that real after all? But for sure: Duluth repulses me.

Duluth spoke:

"No sense hailing a man bent on coming or going. I'll wait you out. We have to pull the area together. Tacoma couldn't come. I'll be your focus. Hit on me."

Cincinnati spread out the stalks on the ground. He took the rock and the yellow paper and spread those out. He sat cross-legged, staring at Duluth. He put the bottle three feet in front of him. Then he crossed his arms and swayed back and forth.

I won't be able to trade with him. He's too locked into his own reaction. If only he would smile I could work this into a joke. Duluth has to get back. He won't make it out here. I want to be back when the sun comes up. What was his name? Flagstaff, I want to have a final dialogue with Flagstaff and then I can rest. If that were only true. The sound of Duluth's voice is unendurable. There is something pompous and puritanical about his persistence. Has he never smiled? Has he never left himself open to accidents? What is this place called Duluth? What kind of rigid arithmetic contains it? He never once lost touch with his obsessive need for control. Drawn by intimacy, he was repulsed by it. I can't look at Cincinnati and I can't move. The soap rubs up against the Dixie Cup in my pocket. Duluth can't bear the proximity of comfort. He would prefer a bench or a chair drawn to absurd dimensions, forty feet high by one foot wide. The path leads straight to Cincinnati. Duluth can look. I have my eyes closed.

Duluth closed his eyes. He leaned his head back and opened his mouth, as if expecting water to be poured into it. Cincinnati read the yellow paper and then tore it up. He threw the rock at the bottle but missed. He reached for the bottle and raised it to his lips but then put it back in front of him. He crossed and uncrossed his legs.

Duluth spoke:

"Call me Duluth. I just moved in. You might remember seeing me on the way in. I'm a steady and located man. You can fix on me. It will help to pass the time."

What is a chair? I haven't been in one for a long, long time. Gravity sinks me down, the edges hold me from too much of a sprawl. My head rests against the back. Duluth has found himself a reactionary instrument. The purpose here is to look down the path. Duluth will stay on here. The chair will corner him. The habits of his progressions will be severed. Duluth will become involved in waiting while I have been waiting to escape that. I sit broken and lumped together while Duluth seduces Cincinnati.

Duluth spoke:

"We'll wait together. I'll put on the orange socks and you can have the ginger ale. There's no fizz to it but it's wet. I can feel the squeeze, if that's what you want to know. I can feel you coming in. I can see those features you've been trying to hide. I've seen all that. You're not together enough to make it cross-legged. No, you're floating. I might have you if you don't make a sudden move. Tell me the truth, you want to be taken. You're just out there and you want to be taken."

Duluth slowly took off his remaining shoe and sock. Then he put on the orange socks. He left his own shoe off. Cincinnati stood, still facing Duluth. He stepped sideways five paces. He stood at the field of ragweed so that now there was a diagonal line between him and Duluth. Half turning, he shifted his gaze from Duluth to the bottle. Then he stared again at the bottle and slowly followed the ground to Duluth's socks and so on into the middle of Cincinnati. His fingers performed part of the Hand Jive. He pounded his left fist twice on his right fist, followed by his right fist on his left fist. He touched his left elbow twice with his right hand, then his right elbow twice with his left hand. He stepped cautiously into the ragweed.

Either the space is empty or Duluth is empty. But both Cincinnati and Duluth are coming and going. It is the situation that has been abandoned. There is nothing left to stare at. I can hear

Cincinnati thudding through the ragweed. He is not crawling. He's walking a few feet and then stopping. Then walking on. Cincinnati's departure is Duluth's separation: he no longer inhabits the armchair or the path in front of him. He can only depend on Cincinnati's orbit. Duluth has to work this out because he's going fast. He's been attached to one image, one confinement, and now the squeeze is on and the image has become attached to him. It won't be hard to leave Duluth. Duluth is empty.

Duluth spoke:

"Now hold on. I can hear you counting. One two three four. I know you're coming around me. What I propose is that we move out together. Count it out together. That was always the plan. I put on the orange socks, if that's what you want to know. Tell me the truth, all that shifting and crossing and recrossing and defining the space doesn't work. Isn't that right?"

Now I'm going to go. I can still get back. Get back. Duluth broke. We can all move in together. I have to keep these words moving to hide the emptiness. When I get up I'll have to go down the path. I'm pointed that way. I can no longer remember if it's the right direction. It doesn't matter. I'll get back. I know we're all going fast, that we have gone, that the only act left is to acknowledge that it's all over, that we're going back or forward, to keep from resting, to keep from sinking down and letting it come. Duluth has run out of operations even though maneuvers are all there is. He defined a space because there was no space and time took care of him. Poor Duluth, he is so easily dismissed. It is because he was so rigid about his mystery, either that or not rigid enough. I suppose he wanted, along with Wichita, to join hands and walk in together. We have all had journeys enough, experiences enough, but the voices are too spread out in the field. They hold on to their own sound, it is the last to go, and the result is confusion and distance. That's a rotten song for you, but it won't work, it has to fall apart of its own accord. Duluth and Wichita and so many others tried to put it together for this last hour when they should have embraced the disintegration of their own voices. There would have been one solid wail and that would have been comfort enough. So say I, holding on to Duluth's miserable and monotonous voice. In any case, that isn't where it's at. It's more like Duluth's shoe lying apart from him, unable to move onto his foot. He would have no more journeys, no more adventures, no more seductions. It is too late for him but that in itself is worthy of a blue ribbon. He might find another finger to touch, enough to sit quietly while the sun climbs above him for the last time.

Duluth sat rigid in the armchair. The steps of Cincinnati moved briskly behind him. There was no other sound. Above him a blue light blinked. The path had grown narrower, darker and he could no longer see the yellow paper or the rock. He tried to focus on the ginger ale bottle. The bottle moved and he shut his eyes. When he opened them he could no longer see the bottle. He saw only the shrinking path. His breathing became increasingly labored.

Duluth cried out:

"You're calling it, Cincinnati. Move in faster. It's smooth out there. I cleared the obstacles. You can cut the circle in half. Don't delay. I might not be able to receive you if you wait any longer. Make your rush. I can't put it to you anymore. Come in screaming and flapping but come in straight. I can't handle jokes or ideas. Come on in."

There was no sound, no movement around Duluth. In the distance the sky seemed brighter, as if from a long row of flames or the first hint of dawn. Duluth shifted a foot, then the other. He opened his eyes. The path had come together. There were no more edges or boundaries for him. His shoe twisted to one side, Duluth bent forward, breathing in and then he shut his eyes, sinking backward and breathing out. Houston stood up. The chair didn't move in back of him. He stood for a long moment and scratched his entire head and chest. He looked at the ginger ale bottle. It was very green. Houston strode forth to pick it up.

Houston tends the store. Houston is a changing and determined city. No soft edges under the heavy humid sky. There is the smell of oil waste and the steady sting of mosquitoes. Growth is inevitable. The port is full and goods move in and out without analysis. Houston will definitely expand. He won't stand the way he does now, looking at the bottle, his left foot posed on the oblong rock, his right foot drawing a circle in the earth. The direction is crude with Houston. It is straight ahead. He doesn't have to sip from the bottle. He doesn't have to leave a marker. He doesn't have to count his steps. Houston is a blunt and fast-stepping man. He's sure to break the cord and summon the voices.

I have to get back now, even though I have forgotten what there is to get back to. I can remember the slowness, the lack of variety. I need that. I need to return to a space I have left so that I can finally leave altogether. I have not fallen apart enough. Voices have not moved in and out without opposition. I still make distinctions. I would have hoped these reminders, these introverted moments would have disappeared by now. After all, it is my isolation that I court. Putting it together simply means arranging the company so that I can take it for granted. And face something else. I wonder. It has been a long night. I'm ready to quit. I'm bruised and weary. I was before it started. Can I trust Houston to take care of it all? I will have to give him a few minutes on his own. He can get back. Never mind the crowd. He can shoulder his way through. Of course, he's not sure of the direction. There have been too many circles for that. The whole necessity for a circle is another cop-out. Tacoma probably knew that. There was a certain dignity to Tacoma, as I remember him. He wasn't whoring after affirmation or even negation. An ice-box was all he needed. I could return to Tacoma. No, that seems impossible. Nothing will have changed with him and I suppose I need that last hope. What is that hope? Is it that no one will be there when I finally return?

Houston stepped quickly into the ragweed. The dying stalks hummed with small noises. Houston held the ginger ale bottle firmly in his right hand. He listened to the noises, as if trying to identify them. He moved his head from side to side and squint-ed his eyes. He breathed steadily. He was even able to smell an odor of old grease and alkali. Above him a blue light blinked twice. An engine droned. Houston stepped forward and fell to his knees. A frog croaked nearby. He covered his ears with his hands. The noises receded. He lay on his back, his hands over his ears, his eyes shut. He slowly moved his right leg up and down. The leg would rise a few inches, quiver and then settle on the ground again. His left leg was unable to move. He opened his eyes. There were no sounds except for the soft tread of foot-steps.

So Houston is involved with his own fallibility after all. I should have known. It's not as if I wasn't prepared. Who knows when I'll stagger back? The brush is loaded with sound. The footsteps Houston heard didn't seem to belong to Cincinnati. They were softer, almost delicate. They were not hesitant or la-bored. I should crawl after them, as I'm not in any way attached to Houston. It is only the relief of not being in Duluth that keeps me relaxed and distracted. Duluth was the opposite of

Halifax. Halifax was content to let space come to him. He never imposed himself but let opposition flow through him. That's how I remember it. I miss Halifax. And yet I am unable to approach that intimate place. The notch has gone up since then. I am unable to sit it out here. I'm too afraid.

Houston stood up. There was no sound around him, no movement. He held the ginger ale bottle firmly in his right hand. He breathed evenly. He took a small controlled step forward. A blue light blinked overhead and he raised his arms, as if to shield himself from the glare. The bottle hit him on the side of the head. He dropped the bottle and rubbed his temple. The small noises began, croakings and rustlings through the ragweed. His feet hurt. He dropped to the ground, kneeling in front of the bottle. He groped for the bottle. As soon as he touched it, he shut his eyes. He held on to the bottle with both hands. The noises receded. When he opened his eyes the sky seemed brighter, as if from a long row of flames or the first hint of dawn. He lay still, his left leg twitching, his right leg unable to move. Behind him, toward the path, he heard a grunt followed by a soft whistle. He shut his eyes again. There were no sounds except for the soft shuffle of a footstep behind him.

Houston has more than enough to do. That isn't the problem. It is how to set up his limitations. The more severe I become, the more that rushes in. I am turning away now from Wichita's fast steps. I'm not sure why Duluth was such a problem. After all, his movements were not too theatrical or trivial. They were contrived but it was a necessary contrivance. Why then have I dismissed him? Perhaps because he never really allowed himself to recognize Cincinnati's features. He was afraid of the intimacy. He copped out at the last minute, unable to lead Cincinnati and unable to let Cincinnati lead him. But he did set up a new tension, a new series of contractions and expansions. And Cincinnati does wander, as if trying to find a place to wander into. Either that or he has recovered his chair.

Houston stood up. Ragweed reached as far as his stomach. He patted the tips of the ragweed with his left hand, as if to encourage growth. With his left hand he held the neck of the bottle firmly, keeping it close to his chest. His breathing was labored and uneven. He kept his eyes directed in front of him, unable to look to either side or at the blue light blinking above him. He walked on, covering a rapid ten feet before his right foot engaged a splinter. He dropped to the ground, letting go of the bottle and grabbing his foot with both hands. He raised his foot to his mouth and extracted the splinter with his teeth. Then he curled himself around the bottle. Footsteps thudded by. Houston closed his eyes, biting into his lower lip to keep from whimpering or laughing. He wasn't acquainted with the emotion that possessed him.

Voices spoke from the ragweed:

"If you swing right I'll swing to the left. We'll connect at a farther point. That way we'll make a complete circle. We won't miss what's in between. Walk heavy through these weeds. You follow me? If you find anything give a shout."

"I don't see it that way. We should walk in side by side, with four feet between us. Straight ahead with no looking around. Whatever it is we're looking for can't be that far away."

"I'm not taking anything for granted. I want to check and re-check every square foot of this area. For all I know we might be doubling back on ourselves but we have to take that chance."

"You make your swing and I'll go straight. I'm sick of you anyway. If you make your swing fast enough you might hit my straight line as I come through. If not, I'm relieved I never got your name."

The voices faded to a whisper and then disappeared. Houston slowly sat up. A white spider crawled across the dead branch in front of him. He watched until it vanished on the other side of the branch. He reached cautiously for the bottle, holding the neck in his left hand and bringing it up to his lips. He opened his mouth to receive the ginger ale. The bottle was empty. He put the bottle between his belt and his pants and stood up. He took a firm step forward but his right leg buckled underneath him. He lay as before, biting his lower lip and blinking his eyes.

Perhaps Houston will have to make it here. I can count twenty stalks surrounding me. I can check those out while waiting for the end. The bottle is uncomfortable and prohibits lying on my stomach. But I was always better on my back. I forget whether I have a hat on my head. I will save that gesture for later on. I could continue crawling. I'm sure I could drag myself a few hundred feet. I might reach the car. Although I would prefer to give it a wide berth. Even broken doors are too intimate for me. Obviously, if we take a brutal look at the facts, Houston isn't going to get the job done. It is not even clear at this point if he has a voice, and if so, whether he can use it. Perhaps the wide-open moments, when Wichita ran to and fro, seeking an avenue of escape or entrapment, are gone forever. He was some runner, that boy. Before that tree stopped him he was leaving some deep footprints around this area. He looks better and better the more Houston sits with his thumb up his ass. But Houston's peculiar stasis affords me a certain lucidity. I can say, for instance, that I have no sense of having come from somewhere or that I am, indeed, going anywhere. I have a spot in mind, to be sure, but that is old baggage that might drop from me at any moment.

Houston stood up. His legs wavered but he managed to stand. There was a small pain in the middle of his chest. He looked over the ragweed. In the distance the sky seemed brighter, as if from a long row of flames or the first hint of dawn. He was able to look at a blue light blinking overhead. A shot was fired, followed by two more. It was impossible for Houston to locate the source of the sound. He took a step forward but the bottle between his belt and his pants inhibited him. He removed the bottle. Holding it by the neck with his left hand, he vaguely parted the ragweed around his waist with his right hand, and walked on. His steps were firmer and more decisive. He tried to whistle but no sound came. He coughed, his breath coming from short plunges into his lungs. His eyes caught glimpses of his orange socks as they pointed the way. He followed his own steps. His legs crumbled as one foot stepped on the crushed bottom half of a Clorox bottle. He fell to his knees but managed to stand again. He walked on. The ragweed was thinning out. He tried but was unable to break into a trot even though he noticed that he was back on the path. He stood still, looking at the armchair. Seated in the armchair was a bald man in a green sweater. He had never seen him before although he didn't look further. The cairn had been replaced, this time with more stalks and three rocks. He stepped cautiously around the cairn, crossing the path as fast as he could and moving into the ragweed. He dropped to his knees to rest but found himself sitting down. He crossed his legs but fell over on one side. Putting the bottle in front of him, he stared at it. His eyes closed. Only by biting his lower lip did he keep from nodding off. He opened his eyes and managed to reach out and hold the bottle with both hands.

Houston heard voices from the ragweed in front of him:

"We have to get us some kind of a map."

"It's too late for that."

"It's crowded out here but there isn't anyone who's in to giving directions."

"It's getting more and more crowded. I come out of Tucson

by way of Las Vegas and it used to be that route was straight ahead. I don't hardly recognize the route no more from the obstacles and turnabout spaces."

There are more than two voices but I can't tell them apart. They shift around. Houston is stopping generally. This patch of ragweed is bursting with bodies. It can't be that they're all trying to crawl into my own original space. That can't be. These must be the last stirrings before the first light. I barely feel the need to mention Houston. He hardly seems present. But I can't remember any of them, any of the places I have been through. There are no reminders, no hidden move with which to trip back into the past. I can only crawl on. Names and pieces of clothing are bound to hang on but I notice them less and less. Something serious must be happening but I don't know what it is. There is only my own momentum and now I have lost that. Is it that I have to begin again? I have to get back. Either that or sit here and listen to the voices. That wouldn't be bad except that it makes me too nervous, as if they're closing in, as if they have something to say.

Houston heard voices from the ragweed in back of him:

"I found tracks over to the east a ways. New tracks but not deep, as if he was sort of sliding."

"I don't hardly know anymore but I wouldn't move. These flats are likely to go for miles and miles and when we get out of them there's likely to be some more."

"I had me a direction once. Followed it a ways. Went through all sorts of terrain. Got so I could recognize most anything."

"We won't see those days again."

"You recall Boise? Now that was a town. The road went directly into Boise as nice as you please. I want to thank you, that was a nice stretch."

"Come up alongside of Trenton once. Never forget it. The day must have been that clear for me to still have it in mind. Well, sir, it was a sight. A man could see the buildings standing up there, every edge recognizable."

Houston stood up. Fifty feet in front of him he saw the back of a man stand up and then sink down. Houston sank down. He had forgotten the bottle. He clutched it in his left hand and stood up again. It was too dark to see in front of him. He walked a few feet and stumbled over a radiator. As he fell, he threw the bottle in front of him. His head landed on the radiator. He lost consciousness for a few minutes. When he opened his eyes he could see nothing in front of him. He could hear nothing. His head was bleeding.

I have to crawl on. Houston might give out on me. It doesn't matter where I crawl to. It's not as if I'm afraid of repeating myself. Something went seriously wrong when Wichita quit. He was gathering his forces together, trying to tie his own voice into those around him. He overran himself. By trying to include everyone lying out here, he increased his own isolation. But that might be what he was trying to do. I might have to spread-eagle myself on the ground as the sky lowers itself on top of me. I have to notice less although Houston is often unconscious. He fades in and out. The image of Cincinnati haunts him. He can't shake the memory of Cincinnati's disgust as he stepped cautiously into the ragweed. That was Duluth. I have forgotten completely about Duluth. Who was he anyway? What did he contribute? He failed to make a connection, he failed to get through, he failed to touch, to smell, to listen, and yet isn't that what Houston is into? The difference is that Houston might not be trying. Duluth tried to make it and shorted himself rather than face an encounter. He needed a vision, a sense of something that might happen and he denied that focus for himself.

But Houston might not have the energy to even deny himself energy. He's lost unless he asserts himself or makes himself available.

Houston heard voices in the ragweed around him:

"You want to say good-bye now?"

"We done that already. You're always asking things that don't matter."

"We come up empty anyway you look at it. It doesn't hurt to roll it out through the lips."

"I don't want to listen to you two. I don't have that much time. Move on without me."

"He wants us to move on without him."

"It doesn't matter. Let the prick face it alone. You go straight ahead and I'll move out to the left or right."

Houston crawled through the ragweed. He heard voices around him. His passage was too intense and labored for him to distinguish more than isolated words. Some of the words Houston heard were:

"Boston two forty... two-lane blacktop... Bird City... Into that. I don't feel you in front of me... Settle down. It's worse when you struggle... Out of St. Louis."

Houston continued to crawl through the ragweed. The light had changed, becoming more luminous. Even with his eyes near the ground he could see the stalks of ragweed defined and separate from one another. The bottle between his belt and pants hindered his movements but he let the bottle remain where it was. An engine droned. Houston kept his head down, his eyes focused on the ground in front of him. Overhead a blue light blinked twice. He crawled around a doorknob and an empty kerosene can. He stopped and smelled the can and when no odor reached him he crawled on. He stopped again when his hand touched the heel of a shoe. His fingers lightly moved across the shoe and onto a sock. There was an ankle underneath the sock. He withdrew his hand and lay on the ground. He heard no voices now, no movements in the ragweed.

The ankle might be dead. I can crawl around. I am not worried about the ankle or what it might be attached to. I am afraid of leaving the ragweed. Houston might not be able to handle that. As it is he can be ambivalent about whether he is really going back or whether he is looking for someone or avoiding anyone. That is how he would prefer to let the end come. He won't listen to the voices. Only banal phrases reach him. He rejects a statement or any hint of anxiety or grief. He is disintegrating faster than I had thought and the process is not drawing him into communion or even illumined silence. It is always the same. We start so bravely with name and vision and it is the corrupt sound of our breathing that we are left with. I can't shake loose. I can't grasp the whole. I have to leave this voice behind but I need help, a caress, even a stranglehold, anything to break this sound, to find the emptiness first before I am sucked into it. Help me Houston. Help me to forget Omaha, Halifax, Wichita, Duluth. I can't lie still like this, inventing supplications, mouthing on separations. I have to keep moving, even if it is a crawl.

Houston felt the ankle again. His hand grasped the thick wool pants. He tugged at the pants, pulling himself up and looking over the pointed shoe at the body and face. The face was clean-shaven and stern. Houston preferred not to notice more. The body was dead. There was no covering on the chest. Only the pants and shoes remained. The chest was thin and yet convex. Houston put his hand on the frozen rib cage. The throbbing in his head and knees stopped. He stood up. He was at the edge of the ragweed. In front of him there seemed to be a flat field. In the distance the sky was brighter, as if from a long row of flames or the first hint of dawn. Houston sat down at the edge of the field enclosed in the protection of the ragweed.

Houston heard voices whispering along the edge of the field:

"I'm crossing in a rush. Flat out. I reckon there are bushes on the other side."

"The best way is to stroll across, as if you're not exposed and you're not trying to get to the other side."

"It's too light. I don't want to see any shapes. There are abandoned machines out there you never heard of. I can't move, anyway."

"I'm pulling out."

"You been saying that since it got dark."

"It's best to walk along the edge and find a corner farther on down. That way you'll always have an edge after you turn the corner."

"We're not going. Too many have dropped. This is good enough."

"Why don't you shut up. It's hopeless to talk. I don't want to hear what you have to say. Hold me if you want, but don't waste energy."

"You go as far as you can and then you don't go anymore."

"There's no place to go. We've known that for a while. We were moving by habit."

"It's too far across. You go ahead. I'll wait for it here. Just go ahead."

A voice screamed:

"You're not going to get me to cross. That's bullshit. Give

me a chance. I don't want to go on. I want to stop. I really want to stop. Listen, I don't remember when I started and now you're asking me to make it to some place over yonder where there might be water and fire and a few more people. Well, fuck that."

Houston crawled closer to the edge and looked out. Even though there was a light in the distance, the field was dark. He could barely distinguish a few heavy shapes in front of him. They might be bushes or abandoned cars. The voices around him broke into a low wail and then abruptly stopped. Houston could hear people shifting about in the ragweed. He tried to sit cross-legged but his left leg had stiffened and it wouldn't bend. He placed the bottle in front of him and lay down on his side. His head throbbed but the bleeding had stopped. His right eye had swollen almost shut. He tried to stare at the bottle. His eyes wouldn't focus. For a moment he nodded off.

Houston is afraid to move out. He needs the feel of people sinking down around him. He needs their sounds and his own sense of secrecy. He'll never get across and he no longer has the energy to work his way down the edge and turn the corner, into another edge. It isn't as if he has lost his sense of a straight line; he never had it. None of the bodies mewing in this darkness had it either. I know that as surely as I know that the open expanse in front of me is no longer a field. Houston might well be ahead of me in the sense that he has forgotten more. He has never, for instance, at least that I can remember, spoken out. Nor has he been assertive. The problem has been whether he has allowed himself to be receptive. If sounds and smells and all the other senses that have left me are still flowing through muddy pipes, then I shall remain here with him and it will be enough to listen.

Houston heard two voices whispering in the ragweed behind him:

"I'm going to ask you something. We been moving through this together for a while. Right?"

"Right."

"Now you know I've come to the end of it. I'm not going to cross that field and it doesn't matter. When you come to the end of it you come to the end of it."

"That's right."

"The problem is that I don't care to wait like the rest of the tribe out here. I'm not in to waiting. I want to manage it myself. No need to go into it more than that. That's enough. Now you don't know my name and I don't know yours. Isn't that right?"

"Right."

"Now I've watched you over a distance and know you have the same thing going on inside you. Only thing is I can't do myself in. What I propose is that we do it to each other. But there's no way without two similar weapons. Right?"

"That's right."

"So seeing as how I'm further along than you it's got to be your responsibility to help me out. And maybe, having done it, you'll be able, with your experience, to get someone to do it to you. Right?"

"Right."

"So what I propose is that you slowly lift your hands from where you have them inside your pockets and encircle my windpipe and squeeze the wind out of it. I want you to do it slowly because then finally I'll be able to feel what's going on. You can have my clothes and I have a knife in my pocket and half a candy bar. Is that all right with you?"

"That's all right with me."

Houston sat up and peered at the field. The heavy shapes in

front of him were more defined and beyond one low and wide shape he recognized movement. He looked at the bottle and then back at the advancing shape. Voices murmured in back of him. Houston crawled to the last stalk of ragweed and pushed his head into the field. He stared at a small rock in front of him. When his eyes lost focus and he was unable to see the field, he crawled forward a foot. He managed to cross his right leg over his extended left leg. He closed his eyes and then opened them. The shape was still advancing. He uncrossed his right leg and turned around. Then he crawled back to the ragweed and picked up the bottle. Holding the bottle in his right hand he crawled carefully back to the rock. He placed the bottle a foot in front of the rock and sat with his right leg extended over his stiffened left leg. He was unable to see a moving shape in front of him. He managed to uncross his right leg and crawl back to the ragweed. From the last stalk of ragweed he stared at the bottle and then at the advancing shape. Above the moving shape a blue light blinked twice. Blended in with the murmuring voices was the low throb of an engine.

Houston has no ambition, being unable to arrive at a sense of going forward or backward. Movement only succeeds in articulating his isolation. He is not attached to the murmurs around him. What, then, advances toward him that he is so hopeful or afraid of? Perhaps it is one last moment of mad participation. Perhaps the opposite, a passing shape. In any case, he is unable to move beyond the wall of ragweed. He sits rigid on top of a rectangle, unable to cross it so that he can inhabit a circle. I can't push him forward or to the side. He has never been able to voice his frustration. Perhaps he has accepted a final position along the edge of the field. He might not be able to leave the murmurings and small shiftings of positions. This resigned collection of exhales and inhales might comfort him. He might manage to accept his own final displacement here. I am saying goodbye to

Houston. I will leave him here to hold the last stalk of ragweed with both hands. As the field becomes more luminous he can slowly break the stalk. Perhaps he will have time to chew it. Who knows, he is already behind me.

Portland stood up and staggered into the field. He collapsed near the bottle. He lay on his stomach, his head pressed into the earth, his hands over his head. The grass had long since died and all that remained was a thin stubble. An engine droned overhead. Portland kept his eyes closed and reached out with his left hand for the bottle. His left hand was unable to find the bottle. His right hand was successful and he dragged the bottle to him and set it upright near his flattened features. He moved the bottle a few inches in front of his head. Grasping the neck with both hands, he slowly raised his head so that his eyes stared along the top of the bottle, as if it was a gunsight. Vague shapes, like giant mushrooms, were spread out before him. A thin vertical line advanced among them. It was a man. Portland slowly sat up. He removed the cake of blue soap and the Dixie Cup from his pocket. He filled out the Dixie Cup with his fingers and carefully placed it upright on the ground before him. He arranged the soap of few inches to the left of the Dixie Cup. He placed the bottle between, and six inches in front of, the soap and the Dixie Cup. Then he crossed his right leg over his paralyzed left leg and stared in front of him. The man had reached the middle of the field. He was walking very slowly, stopping every few feet as if to stand at attention.

There are two Portlands. One on the East Coast and one on the West Coast. I choose either one or both. They are efficient ports that open up to vast and cold reaches of water. Their approaches from the sea are through rivers so that they are dependent on the tides. It is those silent and inevitable turnings that I would remember. Although the intimacy of such an abstract projection is too poetic, Portland might be in need of such a flash, staring as he is at the approaching figure. He cannot look away. He does not hear the murmurings behind him or notice the blue light blinking above. His mouth is frozen, his arms unable to move from where they have wrapped themselves around his chest. I am suspended with him, dependent on an unknown and forgotten proposition. Portland knows a figure is coming on. There are no rustlings behind him. There is a purple robe and now Portland can make out a brown curtain or a torn window shade. The bottle is no help; it has shrunk to the level of the Dixie Cup. His arrangements stand before him, exposed and indefensible. He has established a picnic or a line of defense. I am not able to make distinctions. The cardboard box that has been moving across the field has changed into a giant pencil and now a manila envelope. Portland is not attached to the changes. He has seen six-foot pencils and walking screwdrivers before. He is not overwhelmed at arms made from light cords and legs from pipestems. I am not waiting anymore.

The figure advanced to within one hundred feet of Portland. He stood still, his hands hanging by his sides, his body seemingly tense and alert. Portland could distinguish what he was wearing although there wasn't enough light to see the features of his face. He was wearing loose red coveralls and a blocked Army fatigue hat. He was either barefoot or wearing low-cut shoes. An engine throbbed steadily. There was no other sound or movement. The light had increased in the distance, as if from a row of flames or the first hint of dawn. The figure took another step and stood still.

Portland spoke in a low monotone, as if to himself:

"I've rubbed my hands with this soap and it's a definite feel. This is good soap and will outlast us if you keep it away from water. After all, it doesn't have long to go before it becomes a soft stone. I've never directly used this soap myself but it must have been passed around. It's dry and cracked. If there was water in the bottle you could have a splash and then a wet rub. Then a small drink from the Dixie Cup. That wouldn't be bad. But we're dried up here. We're reduced to arrangements."

Portland is afraid to move. He cannot go forward for fear of a collision with a straight line. He can't handle straight lines. The figure has walked with one foot directly in front of the other across the middle of the field. He should pass within ten feet of Portland. There is no way for Portland to greet a programmed approach. He is suspended outside the edge, unable to move into the field. Portland assumed that the field was rectangular and that, of course, it wasn't a field at all. The precision of the figure's approach has caused me to nearly nod off. And yet perhaps he isn't approaching but is walking a strict line across the field. Perhaps he will do an about-face and return on the same tracks. Perhaps I have involved him more than he is involved with himself. He stands and looks in front of him but he might be blind. He might see only the ragweed. I am waiting but Portland is not proceeding with anything or applying himself to a task or movement. He sits without alibi, without even the coordinating thought that he waits for himself.

The figure walked forward. There was no sound, no movement other than the quiet steps of his progress. Portland was unable to keep his eyes away from the figure's knees as they bent into each step. The red coveralls were tighter than they had first seemed. The face under the green fatigue hat was spectral and luminous. The black eyes were wide and unblinking, the nose loose and drooping to the upper lip. He had no teeth and his wide mouth was set in a wavering yet determined line. He was wearing blue and white track shoes so that his feet seemed to have no weight as they moved forward. His upper body was rigid and unflexible, his arms hanging stiffly by his sides. Portland looked at the bottle but his eyes lost their focus. His gaze shifted to the middle of the red coveralls. The red coveralls stopped and the arms moved slowly across the chest.

I want to hail him. It has all come to this. I want to signal to him through whatever darkness separates us. Wichita would have moved out toward him. But Wichita failed also. Duluth, I can't remember Duluth. Houston was no help. Real blood is needed. I don't have the knife or pistol. I would slash a piece from myself and throw it forth. I need to flay my muscles, to cry out. But no one screams. Those gestures have all passed. They aren't present anymore. The separation occurred before Memphis crawled past the statue. Cruelty could break the separation but that leaves me only nostalgic. Portland cannot admit to any such performance. The massacre sits quietly behind me, chewing the stalks of ragweed before the light uncovers this last secrecy. I need a precise tapping to relieve the fixed space between us.

Portland spoke in a harsh whisper, as if addressing himself to the people behind and the figure in front:

"The edge of the field is absolutely certain. Of course I've pushed out beyond it. You might say it's between me and the ragweed. So that I might not be the space where I am. I'm open for a greater line. Now I'm not sure where the transgression occurred, the one that pushed me out and then allowed me to know I was going on. Oh hell, it probably happened in Memphis, way before the ragweed. Maybe in Omaha but I've been traveling since then. Tired, too. I'm actually tired and this isn't where I'm going to finally wrap it all together. Nosir. But let me tell you, there's water back there. I've been doing with water what most people haven't been able to even get to with air. I'm on the way back now; figure to make my move along the edge. When I hit that first corner I want to keep it nice and controlled as I make the turn. I'll head down the line, keeping my left side to the edge and then swing into the final corner fast. I won't wait. My steps aren't the best but they'll do, you know what I mean? So I'll be coming down the line and I'll make my stop right across the field from where we're all standing or sitting at this particular moment. Then I'll plunge into whatever is there. Yessir, I'm most likely on my way back."

There was no sound, no movement in the ragweed or in the field. The figure stared toward Portland but more over his head than at it. The light had increased in the distance, as if from a row of flames or the first hint of dawn. Overhead a blue light blinked twice. Across the field a shot rang out, illuminating the silence that followed. Portland tried to breathe evenly in and out but he gasped and brought his hand up to his mouth. The air was heavy and smelled of burning rubber. Portland wiped his mouth and then his forehead. His hand trembled and he steadied it by grasping his neck and slowly pressing into it. He choked and was forced to abandon his grip. His hand scratched the top of his head and then his chest. He ripped his shirt and a drop of blood formed where his nails sank into his skin. He scratched on while the other hand reached out and squeezed the soap. The figure walked forward.

Portland spoke, the sound of his voice rising and falling:

"Call me Portland. I came out to sit awhile ago. You might have noticed. There was that moment when I peered through the ragweed. That was when it started to come down on me. I've been through a host of places: Memphis, Halifax, Wichita, Duluth. Like that. I no longer know how to tell it like it comes. But

I've come a distance. I can shrug to the rear, knowing there has been no line, no early stage, no moving degree. I have invented a problem, no mistaking that, now that a problem has occurred. I don't want to smooth out a spot. I notice too much. I should let you notice me. I started too slowly, with all that internal rap Memphis and Omaha were into. There has been a continuation now but I can't sit quietly without a struggle. I'll work on down the edge. It's hard not wrapping it together. I keep trying to wrap it together. When I stop that I'll stop it all. It is coming on to dawn. I would have preferred not to get into this. There have been too many lines, too many affiliations. I'm not into that although I could be."

The figure passed Portland and disappeared into the ragweed.

I'm not going back to Memphis if that is what Portland is thinking. I should say something about the figure passing. I don't know how to. Except that I noticed that I couldn't notice him. But Portland didn't blow it. There are a lot of cozy connections he could have made but didn't. Although I can't exactly feel relaxed with what he left me with. I should move on. I can't return to the ragweed and I can't walk directly across the field. I don't have the confidence for that although Portland might give it a try. The only alternative is to work the edge. If I play the corners right I can make it to the other side of the field and come up parallel to where I am now. It must be a field. If the area has never been previously defined, that is to say, if there are no corners, I am in trouble. There is no time to define space. Space must define Portland, either that or he must count himself to sleep.

Portland stood up. He slowly turned his left foot to the left and then brought his right foot around so that it pointed in the same direction. He took a step. His legs held. He felt dizzy and nauseous and waited for his head to clear. The light had increased in the distance, as if from a row of flames or the first hint of dawn. Around the field an engine throbbed. Overhead a blue light blinked twice. Portland took another step. He could hear the murmur of voices from the ragweed. His bones felt cold and damp. He slowly counted his steps aloud, pausing after each one. After his tenth step he stopped and turned to look back where he had come from.

I have forgotten the soap, the bottle and the Dixie Cup. I need them, as much to have them to throw away as for their weight and proximity to my skin. It is too late to go back. Portland is set straight ahead. If he goes back he might never return. The threat of sitting with his back to the ragweed and his eyes unfocused on the vast expanse in front of him is too much. I have advanced ten steps. I would expend twenty steps before I returned to this spot. Portland must go on. I have to have him go on.

Portland looked ahead and took another step. He extended his left arm to his side as if he was straight-arming the voices now rising in volume from the ragweed. His arm shook and he dropped it limply to his side. He took five quick steps before he stopped. There was no corner in sight.

A deep voice rose above the murmur from the ragweed:

"I'm listening to you breathe, god dammit. I've been listening ever since it got dark. Don't breathe with your mouth open if you don't want my attention. Don't make any signals. It's too late for that. Listen, if you can't take it here walk on out. There's people out there. That's one way to get through it. I'm sinking now and it's a relief. I want you to know that."

If I could fix the number of steps until I make my turn, that would ease the anxiety. The sounds from the ragweed are becoming louder. I might have to create a corner. I don't know if Portland is up to that. There have been no obstacles so far. The machines are probably somewhere in the middle. I am avoiding what is really happening, which is that my legs can barely move, my heart is pounding and my mouth is dry. I am walking without control so that Portland is overloaded. The burden is on him to find and sustain a line. I need a line. The figure back there had a line. If I had connected with him it might have relieved me from the necessity but now I need a line. What is in the middle that Portland is so afraid of? Perhaps an absence of a center. He can't confront the fear of there not being a middle. By going around he can create a middle and pour everything into it. He is creating angles from which I might not be able to escape.

Portland sat down and looked back. The figure in red coveralls emerged from the ragweed and walked into the field. Portland watched him until his outline was no longer visible. Then he slowly swung his head to face the direction his steps had been pointing toward. An engine droned overhead. Portland shifted his gaze to the ragweed. His eyes were slightly below the level of the weeds. The weeds were quiet. He tried to cross his right leg over his left but his leg wouldn't bend. He fell on his side. He tried to find an object in front of him to focus on but there was no point of view. He closed his eyes, as if to nod off. His head dropped to his chest but in a sudden paroxysm snapped forward and swung from side to side. He forced himself to sit up and open his eyes. He stared at the ragweed.

Portland is not able to handle the edge. And yet he can't return to the ragweed. He has to take a step farther into the field or continue along the edge. The voices from the ragweed don't engage him. They seem banal and predictable. But Portland is unable to hear anything else. He is threatened by gravity so that I could easily nod off and never make it back. He needs a shape to embrace. To his right there is a phantom immensity, to his left a collection of stalks that seem dense and uninhabitable. I forget where I came from. It is somewhere beyond the field and yet I can't cross, I can't spin off. It is not true that I am trying to return to an original space. I have abandoned that necessity but I still suspend that loss so that Portland is directed; I don't know where.

Portland stood up and took two steps forward. He looked neither to the right nor to the left. He clenched his hands and set his mouth in a firm line. After each step he would open his fingers and mouth and shout out the number of his step. He was up to thirty-eight. The light had increased in the distance, as if from a row of flames or the first hint of dawn. The air was still and fetid. Portland could barely hear himself breathe. He could distinguish nothing in front of him. His feet were cold and the orange sock on his right foot had ripped across the toes. He reached the forty-first step. He stopped, as if about to fall but remained standing.

Portland heard voices from the ragweed:

"Don't try to make yourself useful. You'll only run out of breath."

"I can measure the space between each stalk. When that gets boring I can count the stalks and then your inhales and exhales. When you stop breathing I can count my own breath and when I stop breathing someone else can count my breath."

"There is no space now. No one is able to look into the field anymore. It doesn't matter that we have become inaccessible."

"Whatever it was, it must have been a fabulous mistake."

"Can you remember how you got here?"

"No."

"But there are still echoes. I find that strange."

"I want to declare something. I really want to declare something."

Portland took the forty-second step. The voices diminished to a murmur. Around him an engine droned. A blue light blinked twice in the black sky in front of him. He was not conscious of the quality of light as he stepped on. His eyes were focused on the tip of each orange sock as they completed their step. The ground was bare of objects. There were only dead tufts of grass to step over. He shouted out the fiftieth step and raised one clenched fist over his head. He managed to take a step sideways into the field. Then he rested.

Portland heard a low voice from the ragweed:

"I'm pulled. It's better in here, no alternatives. I have two or three moves. That's enough. I'll let the flames signal through me. I am soothing myself. You see that. I will tell you a beautiful story. If I could find the words... Ash, how's that? And fresh linens. Eagles and washed footprints... All that won't do. I won't talk anymore."

Portland took the fifty-first step. Then he stopped, as if to listen for a voice from the ragweed.

I can handle thirty more steps. Then I'll have to make a corner. I'm afraid of roundness. There are no more voices. The voices were freaking Portland. They came as if from inside him. He was barely able to walk and listen at the same time. In fact, he couldn't. It is only when he stops that the voices intrude. It doesn't matter. Thirty more steps and he will be involved in a new direction. Portland's steps are fallible to the point of extinction. He no longer suffers separation from enclosed spaces. It is only me that lags behind. I can't catch up to the progress he has in mind or has in some way committed himself to.

Portland yelled out the fifty-second step. In the distance there was a faint glow, as if from a row of flames or the first hint of dawn. There was a shape in front of him close to the ground. He took a step toward it and then another. He heard whispers from the ragweed but the words weren't distinct. The shape was an oil drum. He forced himself to breathe evenly before he took his seventy-first step. His legs wobbled but he completed the step. Then he took four steps and rested at seventy-five. Overhead a blue light blinked twice. There was no sound, no movement from the ragweed or the field. He took two steps and stopped.

Portland might refuse to reach the oil drum. He might have to create his own turn. His decision terrifies me. There will be no shelter within the corner he creates. I need a haven to ensure myself a static interlude, a place where I won't have to talk to myself. I might need a refuge. I am farther in the field than I thought. Portland must have been moving obliquely as well as straight ahead. There is so much distance between Portland and myself. I need another emergence, another line. The fact is, the figure in the red coveralls exhausted me. He threw me into the solitude of numbers. Portland couldn't handle him. If I am exposed to my own steps and nothing else, if the passage of the figure in the red coveralls throws my voice into an echo, then I have forgotten a direction. If Portland is so spaced then I have to play it up. I can't let the oil drum fashion my turn. I will have to let Portland do it himself. There are fewer words now. I might be stalling. I might not be able to acknowledge that I'm spilling out of myself.

Portland took one step toward the oil drum. It was twenty

feet away. He stopped and then moved his right foot to the right, swinging his left foot around so that now they were lined up and pointing straight ahead. His back was now to the ragweed. He heard nothing. He saw only a blue light blinking overhead and a glow in the distance, as if from a row of flames or the first hint of dawn. There was no ragweed on his left. There was an emptiness he was unable to fill.

Portland will take seventy-five steps and make a turn. There will be no hesitations and no delays. He will walk a straight line. There is too much space on either side for Portland to look to his right or left. There are no voices. The loss of a voice keeps his eyes focused on the dead tufts of grass. Wichita, Duluth, Houston, all seemed to encourage the surrounding voices to lose their particular definitions. But they might have needed the sound. There was some heat involved there. Portland feels racked by a nameless separation and yet never has he walked so freely, now that he is bound by desperate control. He no longer is able to shout out the number of steps. I no longer remember where I'm coming from or where I'm going. I only know Portland is committed to seventy-five steps and a sharp controlled turn.

Portland's steps were short and delicately placed, yet there was a fierce determination in the rhythm of their sequence. His wound had opened on his forehead and blood dripped over his left eye. He made no effort to stop the flow when the blood reached the corner of his mouth. The throb of an engine seemed to come from inside him as well as exist around him. There was a glow in the distance, as if from a row of flames or the first hint of dawn. The night was purple to Portland rather than black, as it had appeared to Wichita and Duluth. There was no light overhead, no visible shape to point toward. Portland stopped to commemorate his thirty-fifth step. He sank to his knees, feeling the ground in front of him with both hands. He felt the earth and a dead tuft of grass. He entered both pockets with each hand but the pockets were empty. He tried to cross his right leg over his left but both legs had stiffened so that the effort caused him to fall on his back. Overhead a blue light blinked twice. He stood up and took a step. He continued forward for thirty-nine steps without incident or delay. He walked methodically into the turn. He swung his right foot to the right and followed with his left.

Portland survives. There is more light and yet I see less. It is a relief not to know where I have to go, to let the walk take care of itself. Portland is diminishing so that I might increase. I am no longer on the edge. There is nothing known or recognized on either side of Portland. Behind there is the vacuous angle of an arbitrary turn. In front there is the same proposition. I am the edge.

Portland's steps were short and delicately placed, yet there was determination in the slow rhythm of their progress. The blood had stopped flowing and was caked on his forehead and cheek. The left eye was swollen shut. The low throb of an engine seemed to exist inside of him as well as around him. There was a glow in the distance, as if from a row of flames or the first hint of dawn. A figure in red coveralls and a khaki fatigue hat passed in a direct line behind Portland. Portland hesitated, shuffling his feet, but then walked on. There was no light above him. He saw nothing, smelled nothing. The air had become damp and chilly and Portland's breathing was painful and labored. He reached the seventy-fifth step without incident or delay. He walked methodically into the turn, swinging his right foot into a right angle and following with the left foot. Then he stepped on.

Portland's feet have a life of their own. I can forget them. I accept my words without attachment, as if they flow through Portland. My breathing has become less noticeable. Portland has no questions, no thoughts. There is only momentum, braced and conditioned by a future turn. I am not moving forward or backward. I might be encircling myself.

Portland's steps were inevitably placed. There was no effort or variations to the side in their slow progress. His head was bent to the ground, his eyes focused on the tip of each orange sock as it completed a step. He didn't notice the ragweed to his left or the blue light blinking overhead. He counted his steps in a low monotone, moving his lips distinctly with each number. He inhaled in silence and exhaled on the sound of the number. He passed the thirty-fifth step without hesitation. He reached the seventy-fifth step. To his right was an upright bottle, a cake of soap and a Dixie Cup. He stopped and turned toward them.

I have seen these objects before although Portland might not recognize them. They mean nothing to me. And yet I've paused before them. Perhaps they mean something to Portland. In any case, I've sat down, or rather fallen over, as my legs wouldn't support a sitting position. I don't know what these objects mean except as obstacles before me. I could invent a situation or re-member how I picked them up. I know all about that. But my memory doesn't carry any weight with Portland. I'm not sure about their relationships to each other and to me. I might not have the time to consider it. Portland doesn't inhabit that kind of time. I will bring them along anyway. Their colors are pleas-ing. And there must be more to it than I am able to say. Cer-tainly I have stretched out here before. Yet the field in front of me is more hospitable than the ragweed in back of me. I can hear voices but don't have the curiosity to distinguish in-dividual words. I prefer a hum. But words will come later. I'm sure of that. Not that they aren't already pouring out of me. But something has dropped away, some information about my own passage. I am not concerned with direction. That has taken care of itself. But Portland is slipping, has slipped away. He did it quietly. He did it after the second turn. He canceled himself out so as not to go backward or forward. He abandoned his purpose which was to go straight ahead. He succeeded in negating his own definitions as another kind of movement became available to him. It was the increase of light. In any case, he sank gracefully into the hollow spaces of a turn. But he never broke. He never created opposition to the walk that was going on without him. He dissolved. Although Portland crossed over the edge and left me on my own for two turns, as if to say, I was moving on my own accord, I am not ready to let go altogether. Or rather, I have let go but I am not ready.

Mobile took up the slack by reaching for the bottle. He tilted it to his mouth but there was no liquid inside. He put the bottle between his pants and then reached for the soap and the Dixie Cup. He stood up and put the soap in his left pocket and the Dixie Cup in his right pocket. Mobile stepped into the field. He was aware of a glow in the distance, as if from a row of flames or the first hint of dawn.

Mobile is a fluid man. Particular gestures don't engage him. He is close to the bone, his senses attuned to changes. He won't sit too long or become inhibited by a stare he can't get out of. And yet Mobile is a relaxed town. Speech is slow in Mobile. People don't come and go easily. There is a haze about Mobile, a light smoke. It has always been a transitional zone, blind and yet reaching out. I feel strange about Mobile, as if I have never been there. Mobile disintegrates even as we proceed. I must have swerved away from myself as well as stepped closer. As if to say, I am not attached to Mobile, nor to names, even my own. Names and places move around me as well as inside of me. They are my associates. They are not my associates. They comfort me when comfort is impossible. They light dark spaces when darkness is all there is. So that I am grateful and grief-stricken for whatever banal crumb Mobile drops my way, for whatever steps he takes in whatever direction. I have been led away from habits, as if away from myself, and I will have no trouble in following Mobile because he will not lead me.

Mobile walked into the field. His steps were aimless and re-laxed, even though his body shook with chills. Overhead a blue light blinked twice. An engine droned. Mobile passed a yellow forklift truck. It lay on its side without wheels. He circled it and then continued in the general direction he had started from. The air was cold and the ground firm. Although there were voices around Mobile their effect was that of a low hum, as if they were part of the engine. There was a yellow light on the field and the glow in the distance had come closer.

I could pick out a voice if I wanted to. But they are more together now. There are not such distances between places. I could look back for words to describe my passage. That would be comforting, as if it has all happened before. But we will deny myself that. Yes, we will walk on. I remember a place, a calm place with water, fire and conversation. We will go there and join hands. Mobile will lead me.

Mobile walked across the field which was no longer a field. A figure in red coveralls walked slowly toward him, as if on a straight line. Overhead a blue light blinked twice. The glow in the distance had increased, as if it was no longer from a row of flames but from the first light of dawn. Mobile could barely ex-perience the weight of his feet as they touched the cold ground. His tongue protruded between his teeth and he walked open-mouthed, his fingers clenching and unclenching by his sides. Mobile's left foot struck the motor of a car. He felt it for a mo-ment with his foot but then walked around without looking at it.

A voice cried out and then quickly receded.

I could hallucinate now. I could play it up or down. I could go to my knees or let the words flow into one another. But we don't have time for that. I don't know whether I am walking or sitting down. But Mobile is walking. We will follow him awhile, for I am not prepared. I cannot lie on nor smite the table. I cannot listen to directions. I cannot summon up protective images. But there is just enough happening. I have enough steps left, just enough air in my lungs. I have not listened to nor have I recognized my own familiar mutterings. But I would have hoped these sounds would have disappeared by now. They have gone on too long. Nothing will happen now but there will be no boredom. The habit has been broken, the process disowned. I must have said that somewhere before. But I can't remember practices or exercises. The time for strategies has long passed. Will the figure in red coveralls listen to me? Will I listen to him? Will we, in fact, pass each other? A greeting won't do. I don't have the craft to devote myself to a handshake or a few words. That is an intimacy I'm not prepared for.

The light exposed the collective tufts of dead grass. Mobile followed his orange socks as they stepped forward. An engine droned. The figure in red coveralls approached. He was ten feet away. The figure's eyes were deep and unblinking, staring neither to the left nor to the right. Mobile's eyes grazed over the figure's blue and white track shoes and khaki fatigue hat. He was unable to look at the red coveralls. Mobile reached in his left pocket and felt the cake of soap. The ends of his fingers sank into it. He withdrew the soap and held it before him. He recognized the blue. He dropped the soap at the approaching track shoes of the figure in red coveralls. The figure stepped over the soap and kept on. Mobile wandered away, vaguely following his original direction across the field.

I don't want to let myself think. There is no single point or object to focus on. The focus is around me, or rather, we are all the focus, all the names and places I have forgotten. I had thought that there would be voices. I had thought that I would be accompanied. I had thought that there might have been humour and passion, at least grief, as these words run out, have run out. Even Mobile has stepped away, drifting, as he runs out of breath. But there is still the field to cross, still bushes to find. Is it bushes? There is not even that question to ask. At the least a collection of lines in the dirt, a place to sit.

Mobile's left eye had swollen completely shut. Vague shadows began to form across the field. Mobile staggered and fell but managed to stand and then walk on. He tried but was unable to take the bottle from between his belt and pants. There was no sound, no movement of any kind. Overhead a pale blue light blinked twice. Soft shapes spread toward Mobile but he was unable to see them. His eyes were directed upward at the blue light. He stumbled on a rock. The ground was rougher. There were fewer tufts of dead grass. Pebbles and branches drifted by as he looked at the toes of his orange socks. He stepped around a smashed and splintered wagon. His shoulder and the left side of his head struck an iron beam protruding upright from the ground. He sank to a kneeling position, his head dropping between his knees. He withdrew the bottle from between his belt and pants and placed it on the ground in front of him. He sat leaning against the beam and holding the sides of his head with clenched fists. He stared at the bottle. There was a liquid density to its shape. The green was less opaque. The bottle seemed to be breathing. He bent forward, trying to stare through the bottle. His open right eye blinked uncontrollably. He closed his right eye with his fingers.

I can hear a sound; no, that's the feel of iron against the back of my head. I can't smell. It could get corny now as words, this breath, loses its force. My eyes are either closed or open. That is no longer an intimate dilemma. I can hear voices and footsteps rushing by me. Mobile is fading. As the light increases and forms expand, Mobile recedes. I can hear him hissing to a flatness.

Mobile opened his right eye. He picked up the bottle by the neck and crawled around the iron beam. He crawled a few feet and stopped. The bottle hindered him. He tried to put the bottle between his belt and pants but his hands couldn't manage the maneuver. He set the bottle upright on the ground and crawled by it. The ground was moist and cold. He paused and looked back toward the bottle. He could no longer see it. He crawled on. Overhead a pale blue light blinked twice. The shape of the ground was becoming visible, nearly luminous, as if to say he was present at the beginnings of a horizon. An engine hummed. He could no longer feel his limbs move over the ground. There was a curious lightness to his body. He was not tired even though his breath was coming in short gasps.

It is hard to keep from going too fast. So much has fallen away. What I notice now is only regressive. I had hoped we could all crawl in together. But that strategy toward the collective voice is only another shuck. That reaching out, as if for collaboration is only delay. There are no more delays. There are no more distances between places. I knew that awhile ago. I can recognize nothing as everything becomes available. In Halifax that would have been an erotic flash. We are getting down to generalities as specifics fail. That could be a drag. There are still names to mouth: Memphis, Omaha, Halifax, Wichita. They are around me. I am in the middle. As the gray increases, my own process drops away. There is nothing to observe. There is only the light to receive. There is nothing to choose. I have all there is. There is nothing to go toward. I am that direction.

Mobile crawled around boulders and piles of bricks. Shadows stretched toward and away from him. Overhead a pale blue light blinked twice. Around him there was an illumined glow, as if from an expansion of light. An engine hummed. Mobile was barely breathing and yet he managed to crawl slowly forward.

I no longer know who Mobile is. I am not attached to his crawling form. That is his problem: where he goes, where he doesn't go. I would gladly give him up. Perhaps I have given him up. There is no comfort in prodding dying forms. Let them go. Gravity will take care of them. Gravity will press them into oblivion. I want to say the same words over and over. I want just the sound. I want to fill up what space I am with one note. I want to follow the note beyond my own conclusion. I want a sound that is not involved with beginning or ending. I want to release my own attention to let in the light. There is light. I no longer know how to notice or present an explanation of myself. Mobile is gone. No one will take his place. I want to say the same words over and over. We are no longer involved in strategies of going somewhere together. I don't have to say that again. Let Mobile crawl on. As he wishes. The journey is already over or it never happened. Let Mobile crawl on.

Mobile crawled across sticky tufts of dead grass. Both eyes were almost completely shut. He crawled around the rubble of a smashed statue and a garbage can. He stopped before the charred remains of a tree trunk. The earth around him was scarred with lines. Spread out in front of him was a toothpick, a used ten-cent stamp, a black shoelace and a red cigarette package. Mobile crawled onto a yellow rain slicker that had been spread out on the ground. He tried to cross his left leg over his right leg but he fell over. He reached in his right pocket and withdrew a crushed Dixie Cup. He fashioned it into its original shape with his fingers. Then he set it upright before him. The space around him vibrated with a quiet hum. In the distance the expansion of light outlined the armature of an abandoned factory.

I don't know what happened to Mobile. He must have dropped away. I didn't hear his breathing recede. There was no sound, no whimper. There was nothing to mark his separation from me. There is no one, not even me, to take his place. That is a final relief. He is gone although he never arrived. All that he leaves are questions and there are no questions to ask. The light or lack of light is the only intimacy. I can open my eyes or close them. The ground is cold. I can say that. I can say that in unison with myself. I can say that with a host of places: Toledo, Denver, Tucumcari, El Paso. I say that with no one. I had thought it would take longer. The darkness felt so located. I won't repeat myself. I have repeated myself. The litany isn't in the words. There is no telling. I have told nothing. I can recognize separations as they arrive. There is too much to say. I could bring it all around. My words are still the same. They are still the same. I don't want to manage the repetitions. I know about that. I don't know about that. I don't want to create a conclusion. That has already happened.

He lay on his back on the yellow rain slicker. He opened his right eye and noticed the light slowly cover him.